THE CELESTIAL MONSTER

Two Collections of Stories

Juana Culhane

To dear Carole,
you touched and
inspired me deeply
when you once said
that I was one of the
most 'poetic' persons
you knew.

Abrazos,
Juana
January '09

SPUYTEN DUYVIL

New York City

OTHER WORK BY JUANA CULHANE

The Revelations of Dr. Purcell,
Stories from the Life of a Psychotherapist
(West Virginia, University Editions, 1992)

The Shadow of the Cat-Goddess
(in The Theory and Practice of Self-Psychology,
NY, Brunner Mazel, 1986)

The Headless Toy Soldiers:
The Terrorization of a Patient by Unsoothing Introjects
(in Psychotherapy and the Terrorized Patient,
NY, Haworth Press, 1985)

For Shamus, Brian and Kevin.
For Panama and Lola.

Acknowledgements:
Stories which previously appeared in Voices, The New School University Literary Journal:
A Trip to Die For, 1999
The Chimeric Self, 2001
Adoration, 2005
Nest of Eggs, 2006
Eros in the Doll House, 2007

With Special thanks to...
Elaine Edelman, longtime inspirational teacher-mentor.
Tom Jenks, teacher.
Panama Campbell, Lola Soler, faithful readers.
Carmen Mason and other writing workshop participants at The New School.
Karen Wilder, word processing from handwritten pages, plus much input.

Library of Congress Cataloging-in-Publication Data

Culhane, Juana.
The celestial monster : two collections of stories / Juana Culhane.
p. cm.
ISBN 978-1-933132-64-8
I. Title.
PS3603.U56C45 2008
813'.6--dc22

2008012462

Author's Note

The Celestial Monster, though an ancient double-headed Maya deity, still represents many of the paired opposites of our own modern world—the Sun and Venus, dawn and sunset, light and dark, the grasping-of-life and sacrifice, power and helplessness, regeneration and death.

Book I

Life as Performance Art

Baptism in Central Park   11

Miss Potato Chips   16

The Costume Ball   21

Cuban Circus   24

Adoration   27

By Proxy   30

For Love of the Little Man   35

Twig Under the Door   41

Stone Rubbings   44

Scream of the Peacock   48

Snow Bound   54

The Mask Within   57

Sacred Words   62

Elijah, Man of the Street   64

Triangle in Bermuda   70

Cloak and Dagger   73

Hound on the Hunt   77

The Claw and the Cloven Hoof   85

Down to Earth   92

BOOK II

THE LIFE OF A MAYA-AMERICAN WOMAN

STRANGER IN THE BAT CAVE   99

HUNGER   106

THE FAMILY WASH   109

OUT ON A LIMB   112

FREE AS THE WIND   115

IF THEY COULD SPEAK   118

EROS IN THE DOLL HOUSE   121

THE BIG PLAYMATE   124

THE CHIMERIC SELF   127

SNAKE WITH THREE NOSES   131

SLAUGHTER IN THE PLAYROOM   134

THE WILDS OF SANTA ELENA   137

THE COLD BREATH OF THE VOLCANO   141

SPOTTED ROSES   147

BUS TRIP TO QUINTANA ROO   151

LOOKING FOR THE HOLY WOMAN   158

A TRIP TO DIE FOR   165

THE BROWN BOY FROM BRAZIL   168

REUNION IN CHIAPAS   175

TAÍNO WEDDING   182

THE RETURN OF THE CLAW   188

THE DOMAIN OF THE SYCAMORE   192

FERRETING IN THE BURROWS   196

NEST OF EGGS   199

I.
LIFE AS PERFORMANCE ART

At the age of eighteen Joanna plunged into a pond in Central Park during a mild hurricane. She didn't want to die but she was prepared to die in order to verify the authenticity of her performance. Despite her slenderness, the lightness of her silk chiffon dress, the absence of shoes, she sank deep into the pond. The water was lit up with shiny green particles. It was as if she could breathe underwater or didn't need to breathe at all. Tall stalks with spiky leaves sprang up from the bottom, calling to her to join them in their dance, inviting her to become interwoven with them. Looking up she saw the churning surface—the wind must be picking up, she thought. Little by little the hold of the water wands tightened around her ankles and she realized she was trapped. It was a gentle hold, not like the way Florian had held down her whole body. Had that been part of her performance also? After all, in effect, she had put herself on that stage, on that bed. Here is the prologue to Joanna's play:

> "Joanna, come back, I want you to meet Florian de Narde," Bob called from the doorway of his office as she was about to exit from the front door of his photography studio. She had been eager to leave, to get home, having worked for many hours modeling bathing suits. However, Bob was not only an employer, he was also her agent. Taking a deep breath, straightening her posture, she headed for his office. Florian stood up, coming

towards her, a hand extended, smiling with appreciation as he subtly looked her over. She was struck by his incredibly long black eyelashes; they quivered as they curled upwards coming to rest upon the soft creased flesh above his eyes. She didn't know whether to laugh at him or to be scared. Was he a clown or was he an animated doll belonging to a malicious ventriloquist?

"Florian needs a model to wear his jewelry creations for an ad in Vogue. He loves your photos! Are you interested? Trust me, the terms are excellent!"

As Joanna said "yes," she was remembering a running joke she and Bob had between them—that she was a playgirl from South America and worked as a model not for the money but for the fun of it all, meeting people and showing off her allure and gracefulness. Her height was not that of the top fashion models, her features were not regular but she'd been told there was a beauty to her ever-changing facial expressions, the fluidity of her limbs. She could go from looking simian, monkey-like, to looking like a Madonna carved in ivory.

"I'd love to work for Florian!" she added with enthusiasm.

"Well, we have a problem. Florian is strapped for time. He needs to meet with you tonight to work out the details. How about it, can you see him in an hour?"

"Oh, but I have—" she began, "No, it's okay; I have time to cancel my plans; this is more important."

"Great!" Bob said with relief handing her a card with the name of a restaurant located in a hotel nearby on Central Park South.

As Joanna took the card she could feel herself erasing a frown from her face. She could feel herself stifling a tremulousness from deep within her being, a stage fright as she was beginning her performance, a performance she could only see as obligatory for a playgirl. Without being able to express it in words, she knew that by accepting that card from Bob she was accepting her script for the evening. She knew without really knowing that it was a script of self-mutilation by proxy, self-nullification by Florian de Narde.

Later that night Joanna awakened naked in a pool of blood reciting to herself in an actor's voice, "Born demonic, conceived by sex, never baptized in order that she be free to choose her own path in the future. Was she doomed to go to Hell?"

She was alone, not in her own bed, not in her room, her clothes, clutch bag, strewn about on the floor. After dinner Florian had lured her to his room to look at some of the jewelry she was to model. He hadn't listened when she'd said "no" to his rough embrace. He hadn't listened when she'd yelled that she had her period. Pulling off her wraparound dress, throwing her upon the bed he had yanked out the rat-like object and had plunged into her sea of red.

"Bloody slut!" Florian snarled as he'd stared at her from beneath his flickering doll-like eyelashes.

As Joanna continued lying listlessly on the clammy sheets, as she watched the satin drapes billowing out in the wind, she thought with pleasure of how she must have drowned all those Florian souls in her sea of red. "Born demonic!" she chanted in her deep stage voice. She could hear the swishing of the trees across the street in the park. That very night the tail end of a hurricane was to hit the New York area.

She hurled herself out of bed, into the shower. She needed to walk, to run in the park, to give herself up to the gusts of wind that would lead her to her watering hole among the trees, to the cleansing

ripples that had awaited her all her life,
to the willow wands at the bottom that
would protect her, that would hold her
in a close embrace.

* * *

Joanna yanked and yanked at the seaweeds wanting to free
herself, tired of their dance, needing to breathe. A voice, a strange
voice spoke out inside her head; it wasn't the actor's voice, "Softly,
softly, don't pull, yank, and above all, don't grip." Slowly she
arched her body downwards; she stroked the weeds, she let them
caress her palms, her open hands and then ever so gently with
unfurled fingers, she loosened their hold. Immediately she floated
upwards.

As she breathed in the swirling air she said, "Life is like that,
like water. It can't be rudely, crudely gripped or it will flow away
leaving a nothingness. Life must be held with an open cupped
hand." Slowly she realized that the strange voice was her own. The
performance had come to an end.

MISS POTATO CHIPS

Joanna looked into the mirror of the dressing room table not recognizing herself. She wasn't surprised not to see her own brown hair, hazel eyes and dimpled smile; she often changed into someone else without warning. This time someone in a beaded leather tunic glared back at her with black eyes under dark brows, a beaded headband breaking a high forehead in two, long braids twisting around on square shoulders. For the sake of an advertising project for which she was a model, she had been transformed into an American Indian, into a member of a tribe from Saratoga Springs, that had supposedly invented the potato chip. The eyes in the mirror seemed to be glowing on and off as if transmitting messages to her, pictorial messages that replayed the photo shoot she had just finished—postures that created cleavages between her breasts and revealed the edges of her buttocks. It was the other, not Joanna, who had displayed her sensuality for the past two years since she was eighteen. Exhibiting her body as if she were a marble statue was one thing but acting as if she had something special to offer, something others wanted, was something else; to be a spark that could light up those beholding her frightened her, bringing out a childlike innocence instead, bringing out an intense shyness. Tim, her husband, would sometimes look up at her from his books with his large blue eyes and say, totally unperturbed, "Sometimes I don't understand you at all." Long ago when she was a child her mother had caught her dressing up in her velvet gowns, parading around, talking to herself in different voices. She had gripped Joanna's ear so hard it bled as she'd roughly pulled the clothes off. Her father on the other hand was charmed having always seen Joanna as his compatriot.

The door of the dressing room opened. It was Donald, the Director of the Miss Potato Chips campaign. He put his large plump hands on her shoulders inadvertently pulling on her braids causing Joanna's scalp to tighten painfully. Not noticing how the black eyes had narrowed, Donald addressed the image in the mirror, "Sweetheart, I need a favor from you! I've been good to you, haven't I? You got this great job, right?" As Joanna's reflection nodded slightly, questioningly he continued, "I want you to see a gentleman called Stefan Cedebaca; he's looking for girls like you for a project."

"What kind of a project?" she asked trying to relieve the weight on her head.

I'll let Stefan tell you about it, but it'll be worth your while!"

Looking intently at the black orbs in the mirror, Joanna asked in a flat tone, "What do you mean 'girls like me'?"

Donald's hands moved to the front of her shoulders, his fingers digging into the hollows around her clavicle as he answered, "You know, pretty girls like you, demure, pert."

The lobby of the Park Avenue address to which she was sent drew her right in with its plush red velvet couches and chairs, with its Chinese vases filled with bird-like flowers—orange beaks, green plumes, purple eyes. The elevator with its white-gloved operator swept her right up to the penthouse. As Joanna reached for the gold lion-headed doorknocker, the door swung open. A tiny man invited her in. He wore flared-out soft trousers, an embroidered vest and a turban. She was led into the library where a man and a woman sat next to each other on a leather couch. The man stood up, coming forward to greet her, "Ahh, Jo-ánna," he murmured, his voice melodious, slightly accented, as he savored her name. "I'm Stefan Cedebaca," he added. Encircling her waist, he led her to a leather chair facing the couch, his face close to her since he wasn't much taller than she. It seemed to Joanna he was sniffing at her, inhaling the aroma of her hair, her neck, her baby shampoo and **Blue Grass** cologne. She knew her cotton pale yellow shirtdress seemed out of place in contrast to his brocaded smoking jacket and the woman's sleek silk dress with frog buttons from the mandarin collar down to the hem resting on the carpet. Stefan offered her a goblet of ouzo, which she'd never had before but which delighted her by changing from clear to a murky white as soon as it was mixed with water. She liked the taste of anise, almost benevolently medicinal. Each time she'd drunk anything alcoholic she'd had the feeling she could easily become enamored of its mutational powers.

Without even introducing the woman who had continued sitting motionless, looking like a Modigliani figure, he asked, "Joánna tell us about yourself. I understand you're married and a part-time student. What are you studying?

"This and that, a little of everything."

"So, you're uncertain about your interests, your aim in life?"

"I guess," she answered lamely, feeling herself blushing as she glanced downwards. Something in her knew it wasn't good for her to feel so formless, like an amoeba reaching out vaguely in all directions. Suddenly an energy suffused her, warming her, strengthening her voice, "So, what is it you want me to do?"

Stefan laughed, "My dear girl, don't you know that it's impolite to rush people! I for one don't appreciate it in the least!"

"I'm sorry Mr. Cedebaca," she murmured smiling her dimpled smile.

"That's better! So tell me, do you have any lovers?"

"Noo," she answered in a tiny voice, not even thinking of asking what the question had to do with the project at hand. It was as if she'd always known Cedebaca, the way she'd always known Donald.

"Don't you want to know other men? You're too young and beautiful to be restricted to only one!"

"I hadn't thought about it till now," she answered.

"Well?" he asked.

Joanna shrugged her shoulders stretching both legs out in

front of her, her feet turned inwards towards each other, "I don't see the point."

Leaning forward he continued, "Aren't you in the least curious."

"Not really," and drawing her legs back under her she reached for her goblet. As she drank her eyes turned to the woman, her hazel eyes fixed on the woman's pale blue eyes, almost white, almost blank, except for the slight hint of a twinkle. What was the woman doing there with Stefan? Was she a wife, a mistress? Why was she so still? What did she think of what was happening? Joanna didn't know her at all. It was almost as if the woman didn't exist.

"What did Donald tell you about me?" Stefan asked frowning.

"That you had a project and were looking for girls like me," Joanna answered in an aloof manner.

"I see," he said, getting up slowly and sauntering to where Joanna sat. Smiling he took the goblet out of her hand and bending over he pulled her up abruptly by the waist, drawing her body up against his. He took a deep breath, "Delicious!" Placing his face against the side of her face he whispered, "Kiss me!" Joanna gave him a quick peck on the cheek. "Touch me!" he continued taking her hand and guiding it to his groin. Feeling weak she tensed her whole body becoming like a marble statue, her hand on his body stiff, unmoving, feeling nothing. However, her eyes, blackening, remained alive as they peered over his shoulder and latched onto the woman's almost white eyes, burning into them, daring her to act.

"My darling girl," Stefan moaned, "Don't just stand there, move your hand around!"

The almost white eyes never even blinked. Joanna remained unmoving, but deep inside her a harsh cackle was beginning to surround her soul. Stefan thrust her away slapping her so hard she fell back onto her chair, "How dare you make a mockery of me, you unfeeling little witch!" and as he strode out of the room he shouted, "Get out of here!"

All the way home in a taxi Joanna couldn't stop laughing, a heat encompassing her whole being, radiating in all directions from her dark eyes. Then remembering the woman who had sat so quietly, so passively, she stopped laughing. In the end she'd been so eager to flee from the library, she hadn't even noticed if the woman was still sitting on the couch. What was it about this woman that intrigued her? Was it her light vacant eyes almost like the eyes of the blind? Could it be she'd never seen Joanna at all? Maybe she hadn't even been there in Cedebaca's apartment. Maybe she didn't exist. Then no matter how hard Joanna tried to bring back her laughter, she couldn't. Finally only a strangled gurgle emerged.

THE COSTUME BALL

Joanna had been hired to wear a string bikini bottom and nothing over her breasts. She was to be a sacrificial offering in the Grand Parade at the Ball, carried on a litter by four loin-clothed men. She was to come out as a surprise at the end of the evening, the only semi-nude participant of the gala organized by the Art Students League. The costumes, the masks of pirates, clowns, acrobats, devils, headhunters, vampires, Greek Gods and all types of dancers rendered everyone anonymous. No one knew who the other was; no one cared; the point was to lose oneself for that one night.

The director of the Ball, one of the teachers at the school was paying Joanna extra for the public nudity, so different from undressing for an art class. She was already known as one of the master models because of the length of time she could remain inert, not even flinching for an hour or longer. She would go into a trance and not feel her body at all. Where did she go? She wasn't sure. Sometimes it was nowhere as if she were dead. Sometimes it was to a strange place, a barren peak of a hill with one solitary tree whose bare branches stretched beseechingly this way and that way. One time as she lay underneath the tremulous twiggy fingers of the tree, a shadow had passed over her with flowing arms and legs, a specter that had almost caused her to break her pose. Where had she learned to keep so still even under duress? Her mother had always called her *la traviesa* because of her wildness. Her sisters were at their peril trying to keep up with her as she clambered up and down steep rocks. Her father had had to constantly exhort her to concentrate on his words, his stories, to absorb the world of the adult so she'd be prepared for its travails as well as its adventures.

Joanna could hear the roaring of the revelers from a nearby room where she waited for her entrance. Actresses, models dressed as gypsy and middle eastern dancers, as well as splendidly gowned aristocrats about to be beheaded, also waited with her. All were offered whiskey and soda as their moment approached to enter the Grand Parade. Joanna was to be the last, the special offering of the night, an almost naked captive to be sacrificed to the Gods. The liquor warmed her, causing a tingling in her toes, her scalp. She remembered how wonderful it was to feel the heat of the photographer's lights when she worked in a studio, how the glow seemed to be bestowed only upon her, a glow of ardor, love, perhaps even of a divine all encompassing kiss like one she had never received in all of her eighteen years on earth. She wondered why she craved for these lights which obliterated any person nearby leaving her alone in the universe.

As each litter was carried through the open door she could hear the roar of the crowd rising up like a bonfire at the edge of the world. A pall came over Joanna. The Director rushed over to make certain she looked just right. He brushed wisps of her long hair away from her breasts. Joanna looked down at her chest, no pimples, puckering, creases; she felt like carving an X on each breast to see if she felt anything, to see if they really belonged to her. She remembered her mother displaying her naked body one day before Joanna had left home, about a year before. Her mother wanted her daughter to understand how ephemeral her youth and beauty were; she wanted her to see what pregnancies, childbirth, breastfeeding and hysterectomies could do to a woman. Joanna had wanted to turn away feeling that she was partially to blame for the pendulous flaccid breasts, for the shiny violet scar cutting the lower torso in two. It was as if Joanna had slashed her way out of her mother trying to escape as quickly as possible from a body that didn't want her.

Her moment came. She was lifted up on the litter and carried out into the crowd. As she looked at the multi-colored bloated faces, fang-like smiles, gyrating squirming movements, she separated her long hair into two thick strands and placed them over her breasts, oblivious of the Director's bellow and of the crowd's raucous joviality. It was as if she *had* carved an X on her breasts; there was no way she could expose them now.

CUBAN CIRCUS

Joanna came to, naked, on the floor of a strange bathroom. Slowly she rose to her feet hanging on to the washbasin. She saw a face in the mirror. She blinked a few times to clarify the image—tangled long wavy hair, puffy eyelids, babyish swollen ruddy lips although she was already in her late teens. Then she remembered. She had had a nightmare and feeling sick to her stomach when she awakened she had rushed to the toilet. Of course, she was in Montauk Point for a weekend with Peter, the Art Director; they'd become friendly while working on a lingerie commercial, the one where she leaped around while modeling silky flowing transparent gowns.

Feeling dizzy Joanna lowered the toilet seat and sat down. "I must stop drinking those concoctions of his!" She said outloud referring to the blending of Armagnac Brandy and Orange Curaçao Liqueur. But she knew it wasn't just the drinks that had totally unsettled her insides. Trying to focus, to remember clearly, she cushioned her head on her arms on the side of the washbasin. Peter had gotten on the floor by the side of the bed and had asked her to do something.

"You can't be serious?" she had laughed sitting nude on the edge of the bed looking down at his slender strong body with his penis still plump even after making love several times.

"It won't hurt, I promise!"

"But why?" Joanna persisted, "It's weird!"

"Why not? Are you really that prissy?"

"Of course not!" she declared haughtily, "My father brought me up to be a free spirit!" How could she forget the things he'd given her to read before she'd moved out not so long ago,

Replenishing Jessica by Maxwell Bodenheim, about a sexual muse, and that peculiar little story about a shy girl going into the woods and coming out transformed into a ravishing vamp after being enveloped by a demon.

"Well then, come on, do what I asked!"

Dutifully she reached under the bed for her purple suede high heel sandals, the ones Peter had recently given her. Putting them on slowly she wound, criss-crossed the straps all the way up to her calves. Standing up she tentatively, gingerly, put the tip of one foot up on the side of his belly. Feeling the softly muscular resilient flesh she immediately lowered her foot onto the floor.

"Come on, don't be such a scaredy-cat! I told you it won't hurt, not really!" He insisted, beginning to breathe more rapidly, becoming totally aroused.

Taking a deep breath she fully stepped up on his belly facing his head, precariously balanced, her arms outstretched to her sides, not daring to look down. In a croaky, half-choked voice he gasped out, "Come on, move around a little, do a little dance! Dig your heels in!"

As she did as she was told she felt as if she were getting punched in the stomach by metal fists and as she was about to jump off, his body arched upwards as he let out an agonized cry and she was thrown to the ground. As she lay there, clumsily sprawled out, stunned, he'd crept over to her, caressing her, kissing her entire body, murmuring, "You're so delicious, I love you, I love you!"

Later as they lay resting in bed, he'd told her about the sex circus in Havana, the one subsidized by Batista's government, the one he often frequented while on business trips, where young girls fornicated with donkeys or monkeys, which was only one among many other acts, acts which Joanna had found to be incredibly disgusting.

"I just don't understand why any of that is fun to watch or to do."

"That's why it's fun!"

"I still don't get it!" she retorted.

"Don't you see, *because* it's going against the grain, a downright no-no; it's going beyond expectable human aesthetics, human limitations, weaknesses; it's defying not only our and society's sensibilities but pain, death itself!"

"How come I didn't enjoy it!"

"You did, you did, you just don't know it!"

It was that night she had had the nightmare that sickened her, sending her to the bathroom where she had collapsed upon the floor. She'd actually dreamt she'd awakened right there in the motel room, had gone looking for the bathroom, opening door after door finding only empty rooms. Then she'd opened the last door leading onto a tiled patio like the ones from her childhood in Latin America. The patio was surrounded by flowering potted plants and right in the middle of the vivid mosaic tiles a mother bear lay on her back. Her belly was slit open and three baby bears were eating her insides. Her enormous snout was reaching out trying to ensnare the little bear nearest to her.

As Joanna sat on the toilet seat remembering the nightmare, she knew why she had dreamt it. She was both the big bear and the little bears. She was both the mortally injured and the scavenger, the devourer and the devoured. Though she was in the flower of her youth she was eating herself up alive, destroying herself and she was doing it with a ferocious relish.

ADORATION

The ten women and Joanna sat in a circle on the floor in the Recreation Room at the Women's Detention Center on Eighth Street and Sixth Avenue. All eyes were upon her, suspicious, questioning, perhaps a little mocking. She wasn't disturbed; they were only being self-protective; after all there was a stranger in their midst, from the outside, someone who had been sent to help them put on a dance program by Christmas, a young woman of nineteen who was fulfilling a psychology college course requirement.

"So let's first invent a drama, a story and then we can create the dance to go with it," Joanna began, feeling suddenly too much on display with her long hair, her hoop earrings, her embroidered skirt and blouse.

"Does it have to be about Christmas or can it be just any old story?" Lydia asked with a sneer, her thick black curls bouncing around her brown face.

"It's your show; you can make up any story you want!" Joanna answered, feeling good about allowing them the freedom they didn't otherwise have.

"Okay!" Lydia began enthusiastically, "We've kind-of talked about it; we want to do *our Snow White and the Seven Dwarfs*; we're ten- so, the queen, the girl, the hunter and the dwarfs!"

"Yeah!" Max exclaimed, jumping to her feet, her lanky muscular frame standing tall like a Watusi warrior, "But we want to do them different- the queen is a pimp, the hunter is a John that the girl runs away from, and the dwarfs are them men the girl really loves, only they're gals!"

Everyone laughed raucously, some falling on their backs and

kicking their feet up in the air, others yelling, "Ya! Ya!"

"And we'll have decorated Christmas trees all around!" Carmela sang out, "With great big balls on them," she continued, cradling her enormous breasts. She was the only woman of the group who was over forty years of age, the only one with scars on her cheeks, neck and even her hands.

For many weeks the project seemed to flounder with everyone talking at the same time, but little by little a story emerged and the roles were cast: Lydia with her curls as the girl, Carmela the queen-pimp because of her age, Max the hunter because of her long legs. However, when it came to the choreography everyone insisted that Joanna map out all the steps to recordings of African drums. She was delighted; modern dance was a serious hobby of hers; she had once even considered it as a profession. So, in the middle of the circle Joanna improvised every role, sometimes dressed in leotards with flared skirts, sometimes in full-body leotards with tunics, other times in loose slacks and shirts.

They all rehearsed the routines, day after day, week after week, acting out the drama of the cruel pimp, a flirt of a girl, a rapacious John and seven loving women, but the scene everyone enjoyed the most was the last one, wherein the girl is murdered, stabbed to death seven times by the dwarfs because she wanted to leave them all and live on her own.

Finally, the day of the show arrived. The curtain would be going up soon. Lydia asked Joanna to demonstrate, one more time, in the middle of the circle of women in the Recreational Room. She was flattered; she felt a unity with these women; she saw them as misunderstood by the world, needing to have their intrinsic goodness drawn out. It astonished her that Lydia went on to use her very words when she described what it was she was to demonstrate, "The heroine spins and spins, spiraling upwards, arms reaching towards the heavens, the mysterious beyond-"

Suddenly, as Joanna's feet left the ground, the women converged on her, catching her in mid-air, their arms and hands enwrapping her like a giant anaconda, twisting, sliding, slithering over every part of her head and body, her mouth, her breasts, between her legs. She couldn't even scream. Then, just as suddenly as they had surrounded her, they dropped her upon the floor. As everyone quickly scattered, before the guards could notice anything, Lydia bent over her, snarling in a low deep voice, "Did you think we would *adore* you?"

Joanna lay on the floor bewildered, her silky leotard half torn off her body, her diaphanous wrap-around skirt lying in a heap nearby, looking like her very own flayed, cast-off skin.

By Proxy

Joanna knew it was a no-no to be on a date with Earl, her father-in-law. Her husband Tim was twenty-one, she was eighteen; they'd been married one year and were temporarily living with his mom and dad. There was something about Earl she liked—he listened to her with great interest and she enjoyed listening to him; he was a poet, a scholar, an adventurer. But above all, he had been her father's friend when they were teenage hobos. Her father had been a run-away then and he was now; he had run off to England with Mama and her two sisters right after Tim and she married. Was she angry, depressed, homesick? It's hard to say; she never expressed her emotions clearly, only through metaphoric actions or words. She guessed she got this trait from her father.

So, as to their date; it was late afternoon; Earl's wife was away at a NYC Board of Education meeting and Tim had classes at Columbia University. They were in a bar in the West Village. Joanna loved the darkness, the sawdust on the floor, the cracked, chipped counter. She swung herself around on the rickety barstool towards Earl and then away from him, smoke eddying toward her, the aroma of whiskey and beer in the air giving her a delicious sense of recklessness. She ordered a double scotch on the rocks, just as Earl had done. The taste brought up images of wild grasses from a far-off meadow across the sea, perhaps from around her family's home in England, the one she'd never seen. Would she ever see it? The immediate sensation, from the whiskey and the thought both blurred her sense of self and expanded it, so that she merged with all the forms around her and words emerged with great ease.

"Tell me," she began, "How was it the first time with a woman, after you and Saul—" she hesitated, then quickly added, "stopped being special friends?"

Earl was startled, the deep folds on his face quivering, (even though he knew her father had told her about the nature of some of the deep emotional and physical bonds formed by the vagrant youths long ago). He swung his stool around to face her, his knees touching hers, "It was magnificent! It happened in an empty church on the altar."

"Why was it so good? What was so different?"

Earl laughed. "There's nothing like looking upon a face, the face of a woman—at first fearful, then expectant, then adoring and finally triumphant, and all accompanied by an all-encompassing satiny softness."

"You never missed what you had before?"

"No, never."

Joanna was quiet for a few minutes. Tim never seemed to notice her face; his eyes would become enormous, almost popping out as he looked past her, beyond her, as if at some heavenly apparition.

Suddenly she blurted out, "If you had a daughter would you have told her about Saul?"

"What for? A father and daughter have a special bond, it's the girl's first love, so why confuse her? I've counseled Saul not to tell his daughter about me. Why do you ask? Is it because of your father telling you about wanting me and my rejecting him because of Saul?"

"Yes! May I have another scotch?"

"Of course, as many as you like!"

For a few more minutes she was quiet again, taking large gulps of her drink. Earl put a hand on her shoulder, asking, "Did his telling you puncture your self-confidence?"

She felt like crying as he continued, "Don't let it bother you. You're so beautiful, graceful, bright. You're not jealous of me, are you?"

She didn't answer. She wasn't sure what she felt. She'd been so grown-up at sixteen when papa had confessed his old crush on Earl; she'd felt so benevolent telling him she understood and loved him as much as ever. But way down she'd known something was wrong somewhere with him, with herself; she had sensed there was something papa wanted her to do. Had she thought he wanted her to marry the son of his old flame? (On her own she hadn't even thought of going steady, much less getting married). Had he wanted to show her off as desirable the way *he* hadn't been so long ago? Or could it be something else? Ever since she'd started dating Tim he had been drinking the blackest of teas all day long as he stared out of the window. Perhaps he'd been dreaming up another story, (though he wasn't a writer), like the one he'd let Joanna read, about a runt of a man who revenges himself on a handsome dashing rival (for a woman's affections) by shooting him in the legs and then leaving him on an isolated beach in Cozumel to be devoured by crocodiles.

"No, I don't think I'm jealous of you; why should I be? Papa and I have always been very close, so close I never even had to be jealous of mama!"

But almost immediately, a nagging question intruded, if papa had wanted her to marry Earl's son why did he leave for distant lands? Why hadn't he fought the transfer by his company? Had he changed his mind after she had actually married? Had he become dismayed by what he had done by subtly encouraging her to date Tim and finally to marry him? Had he felt betrayed by her for letting him do it, for complying with his wishes? Maybe he had only been testing her love for him. Could it be he was still testing her?

Joanna kept her glass pressed against her mouth for a long time, then she slowly tilted it, letting the coolness penetrate her slightly swollen lips. Earl removed his hand from her shoulder and leaning more closely towards her, he put his whole arm around her back, squeezing her a little in a kind of a hug, as their faces almost touched. She did not move away.

She knew then, for sure, that he wanted her. She knew just as clearly that she didn't want him. Why had she then continued to flirt with him, to lead him on, then put him off saying the time wasn't right? It was as if she needed to unravel a mystery and she could only do it by forcing the situation to its extremes; she desperately needed to ferret out the answer to the question, "why had her father deserted her?"

One afternoon after school, Joanna went home earlier than usual. Earl was waiting for her, dressed in a flowing black silk robe which accentuated his silver streaked hair, his intense blue eyes, his tanned craggy skin. She headed for her room. Earl followed her. She turned to face him, her heart beginning to flutter as in stage fright. Letting his robe fall open he revealed his neediness. Then almost instantly with one swift movement as he sat down on the edge of the bed, he gently but firmly swept her across his knees so that they were face to face, her legs apart, her jersey skirt around her hips. The effort crimsoned his face, accentuating the deep furrows running from the corners of his eyes all the way to the corners of his mouth, rendering his face the look of a mask from a Greek tragedy. She remained very still. Perhaps she frowned. She thought she meekly (or was it coyly?) pulled away from his face as he tried to kiss her.

"What's the matter? Isn't this what we've been wanting? I've been longing for this moment."

"I don't know; it doesn't feel right, I just don't want to do this," and then calmly, she eased herself off his lap. "I'm sorry," she murmured as she stood up, still remaining next to him.

She would never forget the look on his face, puzzled, crestfallen, agonizingly hurt, perhaps beseeching. Then looking straight into her face, realizing something, his features crumbled inwards; she thought he was about to burst out crying. He looked down, closed his robe and left the room, quietly, slowly shutting the door behind him.

What had she felt at that moment? No embarrassment, no empathy or remorse, not even anger, only a disquieting coldness that didn't feel like her; it was the coldness of a triumph by proxy, her father's revenge upon one who had sorely shunned him.

FOR LOVE OF THE LITTLE MAN

At the age of twenty Joanna wrote a story *Bending The Twig* about a tormented five-year old girl who was very much like her father when he was a child. Thinking himself an exemplary father, wouldn't he be hurt to read such a story, a story where the parents are depicted as insensitive, and worse still, as insensitive as his *own* father and mother? His parents were the enemy he had sworn he would never be to his own children.

The following shows their two stories.

* * *

"Bang, bang, bang," said the boy and the toy soldiers dropped to the sidewalk next to where the girl stood.

"Why did you kill your soldiers?" Teresa asked clutching the tall wrought iron railing that surrounded her family's garden.

"I didn't kill them; I'm just playing. See, I can stand them up again!"

"They're dead; they have no heads!" the girl exclaimed trying to squeeze her head through the bars, tears welling up in her eyes as she cried for the ten little men who couldn't smile, cry, smell the dew or see the clouds.

"What's it to you anyway, go and play with your own toys there on the grass behind you."

"I don't want to!" she answered banging on the bars.

"I don't care what you do!" and he turned his back on her. "Bang, bang, bang!"

"Did you shoot their heads off?" she asked shuddering as each little body went "thud" on the sidewalk.

"Of course not; I found them like this. What do you care? I bet you have loads and loads of toys inside your big house!"

"I hate them all! I like yours; I could make heads for them!"

"What will you give me for them?" the boy asked wiping his runny nose on the ends of his long tattered T-shirt. "Could I have the bear over there, and the clown and the rocking horse too?"

Before long, with great happiness on the part of each, Teresa and Joey had made the exchange.

While Teresa worked out a plan for making heads for her ten little men, perhaps out of the chewing gum she'd been saving for ages, she hid them, knowing her parents would not approve. They wouldn't understand that she wished to complete them, to make them tall, to give them features that she herself would paint upon the gum-heads. She knew her parents loved her but she felt she was not the one they loved. She could not forget what had happened only recently when she'd gone out to play in the hills with her friend Wences. As she'd left, her mother had given her an illustrated history book exhorting her to read at least five pages so she'd be ready for her daily lesson with her father later that day. But only the wind had leafed through the book, stopping at a page, returning to the last one, but most often turning page after page with quick noisy fingers as she and Wences clambered up and down the green and gray rocks. Finally tired, bruised, her long honey-colored braids dusty, partly undone, she had snatched the worn book back from the wind and headed for home.

Before long wearing a crisply pressed dress, Teresa faced her father in the tiny room where all the toys were locked up in a bookcase during study time. As much as she had tried she couldn't concentrate on what papa was saying about the importance of mathematics, history, staying one step ahead of everyone else. She hadn't even heard the question he put to her, but she saw his disappointed aggrieved face as he asked her to fetch the book they'd given her only recently. She hid in her mother's sewing room unable to return to face papa. Taking a pin from a cloth apple she had pierced her left arm from top to bottom murmuring, "stupid, stupid!"

At dinner papa had gazed at her sorrowfully. She couldn't stand that look. She would have preferred to be hit though neither one of her parents had ever struck her. At least a blow would begin and end while a facial expression seemed to linger forever within every contour of the head, the face.

Chew that gum up, toughen it, stretch it, faster and faster, there are ten bare stumps waiting for their heads, their faces. One stick at a time is not enough, nor two, nor three, but four at a time is just right. Four sticks for each head, forty sticks for ten heads. Chew, chew and chew!

"Darling little Teresa, what are you doing? What makes your cheeks so bumpy? What a nasty habit it is to chew gum! Did you pick it up at your kindergarten? Didn't you eat enough, do your gums itch?"

Seeing the carved green box she'd found in a closet into which she'd put her soldiers, papa asked, "What's in the box; is it a surprise for me?"

"No, it's just for me."

"Well," he laughed, "I'm not as selfish as you. I have a surprise for you."

Chew, chew that gum up, there's no time for talk; they've been waiting so long!

"Aren't you interested in what I have for you?" papa persisted, his voice a low baby-talk moan. "Look, look!" and he brought out a red leather book with the moon, the sun, the stars embossed in gold upon the cover. Without opening the book Teresa put it down brusquely on a nearby table, "I'm busy papa, thank you. You'll see, you'll soon see why!"

Finally there they were all in a row, little men with heads, with faces, some smiling with big mouths, some staring with astonishment with huge eyes, some standing quietly with large

37

noses. Some with hair from her own head, long, short and in between, some totally bald and one had only three hairs sticking up on the top of his oversized head.

"Where did you get those ugly things?"

"They're not ugly! They're beautiful, I made them!"

"Where are the toys we just got you, the bear, the clown and the rocking horse?"

"Don't know, somewhere!" she whispered.

"Have you looked at your new book? It's all about the universe!"

Teresa only turned her back. She hated how they watched her all the time with their teary hurt eyes. She was fine, nothing was wrong, she had her little men, her soldiers. If only mama and papa could understand.

One night Teresa lay on her stomach on the floor parading her little ones back and forth, then in circles, knocking them down, picking them up again, kissing their faces or giving them affectionate flicks of her fingers, chuckling as if they were doing something cute or mischievous. Her new friend Joey would be coming soon to see them. She could hardly wait. If only she could invite him into the garden, into the house and up to her room. But she knew mama and papa wouldn't allow a smudged-up street boy to come inside. She put her head down on the warm glossy floor. She fell asleep. Clomp, clomp, clomp! The thundering feet startled her. She sprang up from the floor. Before her stood two giant tin figures with cold gray faces. They walked around in a circle first balancing on one leg and then on the other, their arms swinging stiffly.

"Mama, papa!"

Her parents came running, "What's the matter, our poor darling!"

"The soldiers, the soldiers!" Teresa sobbed.

"Shh, shh, you've just had a nightmare but you're all right now. We're here with you. We'll get rid of those things, don't worry!"

"No, no, no!" was all Teresa could manage to say.

After being carried to her bed Teresa fell into a deep sleep. Suddenly she was sitting up peering into the blackness. Ten giant men stood in a row in front of her. Then one-by-one their heads fell off revealing bare stumps. In unison they approached her, arms extended.

"Stop, stop, you're my own little soldiers!" But they came nearer and nearer. She tried to cry out but she had no voice. She tried to jump out of bed but she couldn't move.

* * *

As a boy Joanna's father had never owned anything that anyone wanted. Perhaps he'd seen a bear once in a zoo in New York. Maybe he'd thought he himself looked like a clown, almost bald with only a few thin strands (due to alopecia), pasty-faced, sad eyes and shoes with cracks and holes. Whenever his mother had seen him looking in a mirror she'd say, "Why are you looking at your ugly monkey face?" The only horses he'd known were old, tired, pulling wagons or cabs or were being beaten to death by drunken men.

Her little father received religious lessons leading to his first communion from the Catholic Church. His mother forced him to pray on his knees and she lectured to him about turning the other cheek when gang members beat him up, laughed at him or called him "baldie," "runt-legs" or "potato-nose." In the meantime, whenever he displeased her, she'd tie him down to the bedposts, face down, naked, and beat him with a broken broom handle, wooden spoons or a belt. His father didn't approve but he just looked the other way or went out with his friends. Generally though, Keith was left very much alone. He began to read, haphazardly, books he'd found in the streets, in the school library. These readings led to fantasies of the solar system, of the Earth as a mere speck of no importance along with all of its inhabitants, while he himself was an all-powerful being. He also read about a world of industrial efficiency, imagining himself as a great industrialist, an internationalist, a socialist, and finally a benevolent dictator.

By the time he'd become a young teenager he was an atheist, finally having to leave home as the black sheep of the family. By this time he was working all day as a printer's assistant but soon quit, planning to jump off the top of the Woolworth Building. Unable to end his life in what he had thought was a cowardly fashion, he took up with a group of young anarchists who refused to conform to the establishment, showing their contempt, their disdain by becoming bums, hobos, enduring hunger, cold, discomfort while they mocked the world, seeing people around them as animated carcasses living on a dead moon with no God.

* * *

It must have been devastating for Joanna's father to read *Bending The Twig* when she was twenty and he was fifty, to see how time in a way had stood still as it had also moved forward, trapping them both in the past as if they had been twins.

Twig Under the Door

He hadn't shown up.

How cold it was. How silent. No one was around. She snorted, lowering her head further into her coat collar. She half-sensed where her feet were going. She didn't care. They could go wherever they pleased. She wasn't even looking. Before long she did look and there in front of her was *his* apartment all lit up. Why not? He was loved, wanted, while she stood in the black night, in the even blacker shadow of a tree. As she began to turn away something writhed, crunched under her feet. Stooping, she picked it up, caressing the crooked twig. It was then that she became aware of a shrunken huddled man standing not too far away. He was watching her. It seemed to her that his arms and legs trembled to her touch, shuddered at the movement of her hands upon the cold scarred wood.

Crossing the street she disappeared into the apartment building. Up the stairs avoiding the elevator. Quietly, quickly—his floor, his hallway, his door. An ear to the door. Merry voices, melodious and high-pitched yelps of glee. A family, a young family. Abruptly she jammed the twig under the door, ran down the stairs and out of the building, continuing to run till she reached the corner. As she caught her breath she sensed more than actually saw the raggedy man nearby.

All afternoon she'd waited. All evening too. Waited by the window, by the rustling silk drapes. Waited on the couch staring at his giant golden flowers in his Jensen's crystal vase, listening to Schubert's *Unfinished Symphony*, sinking into its ominous forlornness. Why hadn't he come? He had called the day before saying he'd be able to get away, to sneak away for a few hours. Had she sounded too light, too busy, though she'd said it would be great to see him? But then he sounded casual too as if any day would do in which to see her. She couldn't have said that not only was she willing to give him all her time but all of herself; suppose he didn't want her that much? She'd be totally exposed, out on a bare limb.

Before leaving her apartment she had ripped apart one of his flowers stuffing the dying leaves and petals into one of her coat pockets. As she walked slowly towards the Hudson River she touched them once again. They were still warm, soft.

At last she reached Riverside Drive. The wind blew upon the trees. They bowed a little. She felt as if this desolate place awaited her—the whirling wind, the rippling river, the emptiness. She stopped for a moment. She was not alone. She heard a delayed echo of her own footsteps. Not daring to look back she walked on, her face hot. Was it fear? No. She was waiting for something to happen. She walked on for a few more blocks.

The river flowed, reflected lights bounced upon it, the wind blew hard and still nothing happened. She should be relieved, but no, something *must* happen. Her hands formed fists deep in her pockets as she muttered, "Come on, do what you must!" The footsteps behind her quickened, grew louder, as if she'd been heard. "Come on, be brave!" she laughed to herself, beginning to walk faster, digging her heels into the sidewalk, straightening her shoulders, listening. The footsteps following her became louder and louder. "It won't be long now," she muttered. Loud, firm, faster and faster—footsteps, her heartbeat, all resounding together. "Come on, garnish this dreadful day!" She almost laughed out loud at her own pompous words.

At last the footsteps were upon her. A presence was close by. She half closed her eyes looking down. What a squat shadow, his was large, looming ever larger and larger. "Do it, do what you will!" she felt like screaming but only a whisper came out. "For

God's sake, don't be timid!"

Suddenly a touch on her body, the merest most tentative touch on one of her buttocks barely felt through her coat. She flung around, eyes bulging, neck muscles bursting. Seeing the same man she'd seen on Central Park West she snarled, "Get away from me! How dare you!" The man recoiled with astonishment and just stood there in front of her, his thin baggy trousers and rumpled cloth jacket flapping in the cold wind. She turned, continuing to walk, her whole body burning; unable to resist looking back she saw the man walking slowly away in the opposite direction, a hunched shadow in the night. Beginning to shiver violently her shoulders slumped downwards, her hands unfolding in her pockets—the petals and leaves had withered becoming slimy and cold. She threw them into the wind, watching as they swished away, falling apart, disintegrating, merging with the rest of the debris on the street.

STONE RUBBINGS

The comforting crow of the rooster had ceased long ago. Dawn had come and gone and now the hot sun engulfed everything in sight. Nothing and no one moved fast in the archaeological site of Chichén-Itzá as if content to make no effort to escape. Even the dust that lifted slightly in a random breeze quickly returned to where it had come. Joanna's arms, neck and legs ached as she stood holding the large white umbrella over the tall figure of her husband as his black crayon stroked the moistened rice paper on the stone faces and bodies of ancient Maya warriors. (In the early days of the opening of the site it was possible to obtain permission to do stone rubbings.) She was as mesmerized by his face as he worked as she had been from the first time he'd drawn her, only now, a few years later, the soul-melting tenderness was gone. There was a narrowing of the violet eyes as if they were reluctant to reveal the flashing flecks within, the effort twisting one corner of his mouth downwards. She shivered. Then she asked, "How do you know where to rub so as to get the original design and not just cracks and bumps?"

Not looking at her he answered in a rich soft voice, "I know what I'm looking for; I know the Maya."

She persisted, "If you didn't know you wouldn't be able to do a rubbing?"

"It'd be harder."

Joanna looked around at the vast open plaza, not one person in sight, only the carcasses of temples belonging to a lost world, a world that had belonged to her mother's ancestors, a world she knew very little about having long ago become a total New Yorker.

Timidly she asked, "Will you be all day today too? My neck and everything are getting really tired!"

He laughed still not looking at her, "Take a rest anytime you want. I'll just get a redder face! After all, it was all *your* idea, the umbrella thing to protect me."

"I know," she murmured, becoming determined to keep her arms up a bit longer. She'd been diagnosed with a joint disorder not long before. "Stress is a contributing factor," her doctor had said, "stress over whether to run away or stay and fight," he'd added cryptically. At the time she could only laugh.

After a long silence, still keeping his eyes fixed on his work he murmured, almost purring like a big cat, the way she loved, "You know, last night your whole body, even every strand of your hair from its roots all the way to its ends, smelled of the mangoes you'd eaten all day."

She giggled. The night before had been one of many perfect nights in their large hotel room in Merida with its rustic wooden furniture, with the whirling fan far overhead on the beamed ceiling—naked, perspiring, lingering everlasting caresses, kisses. Nothing rushed, nothing abrupt, that is until he had spoken, "I'll bet there isn't one person who hasn't loved doing this to you." No anger, no accusations, only a sadness like the sadness within his plea the first time they'd kissed, "Don't tease me. Please don't tease me."

She hadn't responded then just as she hadn't the night before as they'd lain under the circling blades of the fan. His behavior was strange considering the circumstances. But then so was hers. They were both acting as if they'd never received that dreadful news only two days before. "There's an urgent telegram for you, senora, from England!" The hotel clerk had whispered to her. It was from her sisters. "Father died. Funeral five days. Please come." She had rushed to their room wanting to be held by James, to hear that everything would be okay, that the world was still there.

As soon as he read the telegram he had shocked her by

beginning to cry inconsolably; he'd only met her father twice though he'd heard stories about his adventures in Latin America from her.

"Why did he leave me?" James lamented. "He was always going off to sea, always gone!"

Slowly she'd realized he was talking about his own father who had returned home only to die of tuberculosis of the spine.

"*She* chased him away, that fucking excuse for a mother!" James exclaimed.

Joanna had wanted to shake him, beat on him. She had wanted to shout, "Hey, it's *my* tragedy now, my loss!" but she didn't. She couldn't. She could only cry with him as he clung to her.

I'm sorry! I'm so sorry to go on like this; I just can't help it!" he moaned.

She'd thought that at least he'd have agreed that they must leave immediately for the funeral but he'd insisted he had to finish his rubbings. Totally dismayed she'd thrown up all over him. He'd shouted, "What's the matter with you? You're acting as if you've lost the one and only love of your life!"

He was immediately remorseful. Embraces, kisses, hours of making it up to her, making love desperately as if to penetrate every one of her pores, to suck out, to lap up all of her essence. She had later sent a telegram to England saying they'd be there as soon as possible but would miss the funeral.

Now as she once again surveyed the dusty plain of Chichén-Itzá, she wondered what there was about the Maya that captivated James. "You're part Maya aren't you?" he asked in the elevator the first time they ever set eyes on each other, not knowing she was on the way to his studio to be his model for the day.

"Yes, on my mother's side."

"I knew it! I could tell because of the square corners of your forehead, your temples."

Putting down the umbrella Joanna asked, "May I see what you're doing?"

"Of course but it's only another one in the series you're familiar with!" he exclaimed, reaching for her, drawing her to his side so they could gaze at his rubbing as if with the same eyes. Profile of a warrior, mouth open, fierce eye, plumed headdress.

"You see how grand he looks—searching for his place in the universe, ready to fight to assure himself he exists and that the gods *want* him to exist, *need* for him to exist!"

Joanna was reminded that none of the drawings he'd ever done of her looked in the least like her; they had all depicted heroic-looking women, almost masculine, with eyes that looked far off towards the heavens.

"Have you ever done a rubbing of a live person—is it possible to do?" Joanna asked in a low voice that trembled a little.

Turning to look at her, his eyes gleaming with mischief, he purred in his big-cat voice, "What a great idea! Whatever made you think of that?"

SCREAM OF THE PEACOCK

The guestroom in the old reconverted barn was up on the second floor. Joanna slowly unpacked, tired from the long journey from New York City to England to visit her younger sister Ana. Once in a while she looked into the mirror over the wash basin, hardly recognizing herself. She looked so haggard for thirty, deep dark circles under her eyes, weary lines around the mouth, long stringy hair and so thin and pale. She stood in the middle of the room looking around; the walls were papered with Ana's sketches, studies for her statues. She had never seen them before. It was difficult to get to the barn way up in the north of England near the Scottish border. She became aware how out of touch she'd been with Ana; they had been so close before she'd left home at seventeen. Hurriedly she freshened her face, changed into an embroidered long Mexican dress and because of her stiff, swollen knees she baby-stepped down the narrow staircase to the vast living-room below.

It was getting extremely dark and though Ana was nowhere to be seen Joanna had the feeling that she was not alone. A cold draft and the stone floor caused twinges of pain in her inflamed ankles, something like a minuscule electric wave touching her from afar. She thought she sensed presences around her, probably only Ana's statues. She longed for her husband's all encompassing arms, so protective with their possessive passion, giving her a certitude of belonging, of being anchored.

Suddenly Ana burst through a tall arched doorway carrying logs for a fire. "It's so good to have you all to myself though I'm surprised James has let you out of his sight even for a long weekend! My Bruce is visiting his family in Wales."

Joanna laughed, feeling warmer even before the wood was aflame, even before they were seated opposite each other drinking rum and ginger beer.

"I have a surprise for you," Ana exclaimed, "I'm just waiting for a blacker darkness and then I'll show you!"

Joanna couldn't imagine how the darkness around them just a few feet from the golden glow of the fire could be any darker.

She was astonished how by firelight Ana looked so much like their mother when she had been young. Before long Ana sprang up, her sweater dress pulling a little around her voluptuous bosom, her thick wavy black hair springing out from under the decorative comb on the back of her head. As she pranced across the room in her clogs to an elaborate array of light switches Joanna remembered how long ago in their teens they had danced Polkas, swinging wildly round and round holding on to each other's waists.

As all the lamps and spotlights were ignited they were surrounded by looming life-size stone figures. Standing up, Joanna exclaimed, "Ana, I hadn't realized how enormous your statues were!" They were surrounded by women holding babies in their *rebosos*, skeletons in hooded cloaks, a king frog, a jaguar that seemed to be padding about, his tail up in the air.

"Do you see my golden totem pole?" Ana asked enthusiastically. "It's really a *ceiba* tree."

Joanna nodded with recognition remembering their mother telling them how their Maya ancestors thought it was the first tree, the very first living being in the whole world, the goddess mother of all.

"God, it's all so beautiful, Ana!" she exclaimed, making a motion as if to clap her hands but not making a sound, her curved arthritic fingers preventing her palms from coming together.

Ana pulled another switch saying, "Look up!" and rushing back to where Joanna stood she put an arm around her shoulders.

Looking up at the alcove as it became flooded with light Joanna saw a giant apparition standing on tiptoe, a face with a beak, a head full of flowing plumes, winged arms and feathered legs, a cross between a quetzal bird and a peacock. It must have been the presence she'd sensed as she had descended the stairs. She began to sway as Ana tightened her hold on her shoulders. It was as if Joanna were back in the Yucatan. It was as if it were two years earlier when she had heard the shrillness emanating from a rotating peacock, its' feathered skirts unfurling, when she had heard the scream that had heralded the death of their father, the scream that had seemed to say, "Look at me, pay attention, I am screaming for you!"

"Are you okay?" Ana whispered.

"Yes, yes," but all she could think about was the telegram from England about their father's death when she and James had been vacationing in Mexico. Every day after that until they had boarded a plane in order to attend the funeral in England she had heard the scream admonishing her, warning her about something. She didn't know what, but her body seemed to know. She'd gotten an enormous flare-up of her rheumatoid arthritis.

Soon Ana and Joanna were seated for dinner, eating out of plates their mother had made. Joanna remembered how marvelous it had been to have her mother come to stay with her and James after their father's funeral. As they had shared their loss they were close the way they hadn't been since she was a child. It had been good to once again be held by her, to sink into the fullness of her body, her relaxed breasts and belly, not feeling a bone anywhere, her fluffiness smelling of fresh sweat in the sunlight.

"By the way," Ana began, "I have something else to show you, something very special, but it's not ready yet, soon, before you leave. It's out back in my studio."

"How can you top what you've already shown me?" Joanna laughed.

"Oh, you'll see! It has to do with you and me! I started it two years ago right after Papa's death. I guess it was *my* way of dealing with it all."

Joanna nodded approvingly saying, "And I just got sick!"

"Mama told me how your arthritis got so bad you had to soak in a tub for a couple of hours before you could even get ready to go to work!"

Joanna nodded, feeling a sense of shame as if she could control her illness, as if she had gotten it on purpose so she would be pampered.

"What are the doctors doing for you?"

"The same old thing, anti-inflammatory medication," Joanna answered wearily.

"Have they told you more about what causes it?"

Joanna's voice had a tinge of irritability in it as she answered, "As I've said before, it's a bit of genetics plus a hit and run virus, low resistance to infections, and all triggered by some kind of emotional trauma."

"I'm sorry," Ana began, reaching for her arm, patting it softly, "I know you hate to talk about it."

Joanna laughed, "It's ironic—I know, I tend to put blinders on and guess what, the doctor says that the stress created by not knowing whether to fight or to run away wears the body down!"

Ana rushed over to her, embracing her, "Oh, I so wish we all lived at least in the same country!"

Later that night Joanna left her room to go to the bathroom. While washing her hands she looked out of the window facing the backyard. She saw the little house that must be Ana's studio among the somber black trees. Something large stood by one of the windows illuminated by an eerie blue light. It was a tall shrouded figure, probably the surprise Ana had for her. For a moment she thought she saw the figure toss its hooded cloak to one side and straighten up.

For the next two days they took short walks, they looked at family albums, they talked of their experiences growing up in

Central America, whether it was better to be Papa's pet as Joanna had been or Mama's favorite as their younger sister had been, or to be in the middle, like Ana, belonging to neither father nor mother. They talked of their boyfriends, their lovers and then finally they talked of what a strange coincidence it had been that Joanna had come down with her disease not long after first falling in love with James when she was twenty-four. They wondered how it was possible that love be so deadly. Then Joanna had startled both of them by saying that it was the madness of love that was deadly, how it unearthed first love, ambivalent love, lost love, all of love, even love betrayed. She hadn't been able to explain why she'd said this.

It was finally Joanna's last day. She'd be leaving early the next morning. Ana was frisky, mischievous at breakfast, finally saying, "Okay, let me show you what I promised! It's not finished as I told you but I'll show it to you anyway!" Then, springing up, she took Joanna's arm but she couldn't budge, her legs wouldn't move. Ana squatted a little in front of her, knees apart and then placing both arms around Joanna's waist, she lifted her off the stool and led her towards the back door, half carrying her.

As they moved down the narrow stone path leading to the little house Joanna's legs slowly regained some strength. Stepping inside she saw the shrouded figure she'd seen from the upstairs window. Tearing the canvas off, Ana stepped back, looking at her sister triumphantly. There stood an abstract structure over six feet tall towering over both of them. As Joanna's stepped in close for a better look at the shiny marble she saw that the structure consisted of two figures, side by side, their heads turned to face each other, fingers intertwined, long hair flowing from one to the other, short skirts, halter tops, tiny budding breasts, long skinny legs and knobby knees as seen in colts. Young girls, she thought. She stepped in even closer and looked upwards at the faces. She saw Ana and herself, eyes wide open with mirth, smiling, perhaps laughing.

"See, I don't believe in working stone to find the spirit within. I take a spirit and put it into my stone. This way I can fool myself into thinking that no one can leave me. You see what I mean? You leave tomorrow once again but in a way you'll still be here with me!"

Joanna continued to stare, a constricting armor enwrapping and enshrouding her from the neck to the toes. She was once again in the throes of one of her flare-ups. She sighed, too tired to fight, having only enough energy to accept the onslaught, to become one with it. She sank into the pain, the ever-growing rigidity, forcing it to give way just a little and then a little more. Had she buried *her* lost loved ones within herself? Was she herself a stone tomb, a graveyard, so she could possess others forever?

Snow Bound

As Joanna told the therapy group that she and James had fallen in love with each other *before* they met, a young woman to her left in the circle of chairs muttered, "Yeah! Yeah!," and a scruffy long-haired man sitting directly opposite exclaimed, "Give me a break!"

After the leader cautioned the group not to say anything until Joanna finished, Joanna went on to say how she and James had met as artist and model, how she'd studied his face while he drew loving his glowing deep violet eyes, the soft curves of his nostrils, his delicate sensuous lips as they almost opened in a smile. His squarish hand had seemed to be tracing large circles as it drew swiftly, pressing deeply into the paper. She knew before she even looked at his drawings that they wouldn't look like her, that they would be bigger-than-life, heroic-looking. She felt she was inspiring him in a way that oddly enough she well understood; she was to be an ideal and, in turn, she would win his worship. This is what she had attempted to do with her father ever since she had been a child. This is what she had learned, what she had been taught to do.

As Joanna continued telling her story to the group she glanced downwards more and more avoiding noticing their expressions, their reactions. She described their first passionate kiss, how he'd said, "Don't tease me!" revealing to her that she had to be the banquet that didn't turn out to be poisoned, the boulder that never rolled back downhill after being pushed upwards.

"But alas!" she said with tears in her eyes, "I became as bad as his tormented rejecting mother, failing him the same way she had, and so after being together for ten years we've decided on a trial separation."

Suddenly something hit her hard in the middle of her forehead; a crumpled up cigarette wrapper fell into her lap as the scruffy man across the circle shouted at her, "I'm sorry for throwing that at you, but I've never heard so much shit in my whole life!"

At first Joanna was so stricken she couldn't move. Then without saying another word she got up and left the room. Once downstairs she grabbed her coat and went out into the snowy hills of Vermont where the weekend marathon was being held.

Buttoning her coat she trudged uphill into the woods, tears cascading down her face. Upon reaching the top she embraced the nearest tree, kissing the bark, pressing herself against it as if it were the legs of a grown-up and she was small. She almost expected a branch to reach down and embrace her back. Walking along the crest of the hill she finally stopped to rest on a tree stump. Picking up a handful of crisp snow she held it to her face enjoying how it soothed her burning skin, until creeping down under her coat collar it chilled her right through her turtleneck sweater.

After walking for many hours she reached the other side of the hill and there was nowhere else to go except downhill. Sliding all the way down, her legs and feet getting thoroughly soaked, she landed practically inside a shed at the bottom. It was a windowless tool shack totally open on one side sitting by the side of a road. She crept into a far corner and finding an old unraveling wicker chair, she sank into it.

As she looked around, becoming more and more sleepy, she thought to herself that this was a perfect place wherein to be found. Somehow she knew that the scruffy man was already leading a search party. She laughed out-loud the way she had not for a very long time, deeply, from the core of her being. Yes, it was a perfect place to be found, in a dark out-door closet in the blinding snow, supported by a cast-off chair, surrounded by axes, old saws and plenty of shovels. It was another version of the dark closet she'd disappeared into to escape her husband's despair and anger after her father's death.

As she began to fall asleep her mind sped far ahead to the large living room in the house in which they were all staying that weekend, a comfortable family home. She could feel the warmth of the enormous flames in the wood-burning fireplace. She could hear the happy, ironic laughter all around her as they talked of what had driven her away into the cold outdoors. She could feel the embrace of the scruffy man who was really handsome underneath his long hair and unshaven face as he ardently apologized to her.

After all her only sin was that she was out-of-step, out-of-place, a grand romantic of yore. But even in her half dreaming state she knew there was something seriously amiss within her, something that eluded her even after her psychiatrist had conveyed his impression of her as someone imprisoned behind glass, unable to move, to speak, unable to express feelings, able only to watch people go by and to be watched by them. *Now* she understood what he meant.

THE MASK WITHIN

As Joanna sat in the garden bar of her hotel she wondered why the longing she had had to see two statutes in the Cairo Museum resembled a form of homesickness. She had seen pictures of these statues in an art book belonging to James her estranged husband; both came from tombs early in history, both were made of wood and were painted; one was a turquoise woman with bewildered-looking eyes outlined in black, arms folded across the chest, thighs pressed tightly together; the other was a black woman, long robes and limbs outlined in yellow, the face blank, featureless. But now she would never see these two women. The Cairo Museum was closed, glass cases empty, taped up, and the antiquities shipped elsewhere for safety. It was the late 1960s and Egypt was still in conflict with Israel though the travel agency in England had assured her the strife had ended.

"Hello, my name is Rafid," a deep voice began close by her side, "I would like to make your acquaintance if it's to your liking."

Amused by his courtliness she turned around and came face-to-face with large brown eyes, "My name is Joanna."

"You're not English as I'd thought. May I ask where you're from—you have a slight Spanish accent, from Spain?"

"No, New York but my mother is from Mexico and I grew up in Central America." There she went again, divulging too much! Was she being seductive? No. Except for the luminous eyes Rafid was not her type, too short, a little paunchy, around her age, middle thirties. She liked more mature men, tall big-chested like James, men who made her feel protected.

"Are you here to forget or to remember something?" Rafid

asked softly, "I've seen you sitting in the garden for several days now looking as if you've been transplanted from another garden, as if you're needing yet another place for your roots.

Feeling infused with a warmth by Rafid's words, almost as if caressed, she ordered another scotch with fresh orange juice before answering, "Oh, so you've been watching me!" Even as she said this she knew she shouldn't have. She knew it would look as if she were flirting with Rafid, leading him on.

"I couldn't help but notice you," Rafid answered with a knowing smile, "You are very attractive, different."

After a moment of silence, turning around on her high chair to face Rafid, she blurted out, "You look as if you want to ask me something."

Motioning to the bartender to refill his glass mug with mint tea, Rafid asked, "What are you looking for in my country; is it connected with your work?"

"Oh no, I'm a school teacher, just traveling."

"Are you working for the American government?"

"Oh no, I just teach."

Not smiling, fixing his eyes directly on hers Rafid exclaimed, "You could still be working for the American government, couldn't you?"

She frowned, pouting, "What makes you ask?"

"Forgive me but your frankness seems meant to confuse."

"I don't understand, what do you mean?"

"You're unusual, somehow a little strange."

"What does that have to do with my work, with my travels?"

"You are not what you seem to be!"

Bursting out laughing she playfully covered half of her face with her long hair, "Are you calling me an impostor, a liar?"

"No," Rafid muttered, "you're more subtle than that."

Joanna turned back to face the bar, their conversation seemingly at an end for now.

That night she couldn't sleep. She kept thinking of another

woman having her name, not Joan of Arc but Pope Joan of the ninth century. That Joan had been the illegitimate daughter of a herder of geese in England; she died when Joan was eight. Then her pseudo father, a defrocked, castrated, scholarly monk who had lived with her mother taught Joan how to make a living as the two of them traveled throughout Europe. He taught her many things, from performing as a dancing bear to answering questions for handouts as if she were a live encyclopedia. When he died Joan began to dress as a man, as a scholar, as a monk. Eventually she gained so much respect and acclaim that she became The Holy Father, the Pope. Finally Joanna was able to sleep as she contemplated Pope Joan's sense of triumph.

Soon after their conversation at the bar Rafid calmly told her that though he and his office didn't know what she was up to, she was under investigation, that she must stay close to the hotel until her flight back to England in three days. For the first time on that trip she'd felt apprehensive but not enough to obliterate her compulsion to see what would happen next. So, that evening she took a taxi to an out-of-the-way restaurant located in the heart of Cairo. Driving through endless dark alleyways they finally arrived at a spot that looked like Rick's Café Americaine in the movie *Casablanca*, large, lit up, glamorously dressed people going in and out. She felt she belonged (in her black silk chiffon dress, a lace hooded cape covering her from her upswept hair to her beaded satin pumps), looking like a woman in one of Goya's dark paintings.

Everyone ate at communal tables while seated on low silk-padded stools, using gold utensils and drinking rich red wines from gold goblets. From what she could see and hear she was the only American among Africans, Spanish, Italians, Scandinavians and Eastern Europeans. She communicated with everyone by speaking Spanish and by understanding French and Italian. Platters of meat, vegetables and fruits were placed in front of them. Then one of the waiters offered her a special dish, "a gift from the house," he murmured in her ear, squabs encrusted in a golden honeyed herbal coating. Feeling flattered and loving the oregano flavor she ate all three of the tiny delicate birds.

Joanna didn't remember anything further. She awakened the next day in an opulent tent, a young man sitting by her side. She was dressed in her own pajamas. Her luggage was nearby. As she sat up on her couch the young Nubian handed her a sheet of plain white paper, a message within, typed, not signed, "Madame, you're in the desert. Your caretaker's name is Laith and he speaks only Arabic. He will cook, clean and wash-up for you, even entertain you, but you are not to leave the tent. At dawn on Monday you'll be transported to the airport for your flight."

Her skin began to ripple as everything within her speeded up, her pulse, the flow of blood. Seldom in her life had she felt such an enhancement of life's forces. Was she going to be murdered, made to disappear forever? By Laith? Glancing at him it was hard to believe he could kill anyone—clear open face, handsome head crowned by a gold and blue turban, crisp white caftan. But as she looked more closely she noticed he had a curved dagger secured in his red sash around his pelvic area. Should she scream, try to run out, die fighting for her life? No, she was consumed by an acute inquisitiveness as to what would happen if she just watched the exhibit that was herself, if she became both the seer and the seen, the voyeur and the exhibitionist. Calmed by this distancing she looked around her. There was a sitting area full of giant cushions, folding ivory-enameled tables, screens and drapes everywhere half hiding the burner, icebox, enormous bottles of water, a commode and even a full array of gleaming copper pots including one large enough for a sponge bath. Would Rafid and his colleagues have gone to so much trouble if they were planning to do away with her? Turning back to look at Laith she noticed he hadn't moved, his eyes fixed on hers, questioning, as if waiting for instructions. Sitting up even more upright, puffing up the cushions behind her, Joanna smiled at him. He rose to his feet, beginning to sway, undulate, as a dolorous song flowed from his barely opened lips, a blending of the flamenco '*grito hondo*' and an African warrior's melody of death. Slowly he speeded up till he lost his outline, becoming only a gyrating inverted funnel of colors, brown, gold, white, dots of crimson. Soon she felt as if she were the one whirling about, as if she were the one in an ecstatic delirium losing herself to a higher power, not caring if these were to be the last moments of her life, all the while also aware that she was merely a spectator. Suddenly pieces of clothing went flying into the air, soon falling to the floor, the turban, the sash, the caftan, no sign of the dagger—it must have flown onto a cushion in a far off corner. All movement came to a stop and there before her crouched a naked deep brown body with long black hair, a lean nimble-limbed figure that slowly stood erect in front of her. It was a young woman, very young with barely budding breasts, a few curls upon her pubus. As Joanna stood staring with awe, surprise, the dancer began to laugh the laugh of the most triumphant of all souls. But her voice was deep like a man's, turning her laughter into a hard-hitting weapon.

As Joanna continued sitting, her head bowed in shock, she knew with certainty that Rafid himself was conveying a message to her through Laith. Once again he was telling her she was not for real, that she was not what she seemed, that she was double-faced possessing a forked tongue, in short that she was an imposter. Why would he go to so much trouble? Surely he didn't believe she was dangerous. Perhaps it was personal.

Finally becoming alert she noticed the naked Laith going through her suitcase. Picking out a lavender pantsuit she disappeared into a corner with it, chuckling to herself with great contentment, her face deformed by the smirk of gloating.

Suddenly Joanna felt a great emptiness, the emptiness of the deflated, the foolish. She was now just a woman, alone and helpless. She was no longer the exhibit that was herself. She was no longer the seer and seen. What was she? Who was she?

SACRED WORDS

Joanna hated hospitals ranging back over thirty-five years of adult life, multiple joint reconstructions and replacements, a total hysterectomy, still further surgery to remove a malignancy in the colon. However, she *had* to visit her husband James when he was hospitalized after he had a series of strokes, slipping into a coma but still able to breathe on his own.

She visited every day, staying all day. Sometimes she'd go out briefly to an Irish Pub, on East 70th Street, called *The Recovery Room* and drink to their long marriage, to both the good and the bad within it, including a long separation. One week went by. Then two more. She cried over him, kissing his still rounded pink cheeks and read the whole of Sean O'Casey's autobiography to him. One day she blurted out unexpectedly, "I've loved you from the moment I saw you in your floppy beret, your bright-colored shirt and your baggy pants, your eyes constantly twinkling. Then as the years passed, I loved your padding about with the grace and power of a lion. Now you are my tattered lion and I will remain with you forever. Believe me and survive; believe my love and awaken."

Then, one day, she stood by the swinging door leading to James' ward, looking through the glass pane, wondering how many more times she could bear to enter through it. Finally as she slowly pushed the door open, the nurse came running down the hall to greet her, "He's awake, he's awake!" Joanna rushed to his room. His eyes were open but they expressed total bewilderment. Then, seeing her, he picked his head up a little, raised his arms weakly, and smiled the smile of a pixie. As Joanna embraced him, kissing his face fervently, he murmured, "I was having the most marvelous dream!" But before he could continue, the nurse interceded with excitement, "I was washing his privates and he suddenly said, 'Hey, watch it; I'm a married man you know!'" Joanna laughed; the incident was just like one of the many funny stories, jokes really, that James was always telling.

After puttering around him drawing blood, checking his vitals and his intravenous nourishment, the staff went away smiling with satisfaction.

"Tell me about your dream," Joanna said, wondering if her words to him had had some effect on him. Eagerly James began to tell her how he and the great General Alcibiades of ancient Greece had walked together in the Agora, the main square, how his hospital sheet wrapped around him had looked no less elegant then the flowing robes Alcibiades was wearing, and how his own tiara of white hair, looking like albino leaves, surrounding his bald pate, was just as regal as the golden leaves upon the young general's head. Then with surprising energy, James went on to describe how, side by side, they had then sneaked into a procession on a sacred road in Eleusis, leading to an altar where Demeter, the Goddess of Grain, would merge with Pluto, the giver of all the fruits of the earth. James desperately wanted to hear what mysteries the high priest was unveiling to the initiates as they were blessed and garlanded. But he couldn't hear the secret words. Then Alcibiades had whispered into his ear, "There is nothing to learn, nothing to do, only something to experience, and once you do, you will never again be afraid of death."

Joanna was in awe, not only of his dream but of James' ecstatic reaction to it; his whole face glowed. She kissed him fully on his lips, so happy for him, for her, for them. But then, she had to restrain herself. She had actually felt like biting into his lip. Besides hospitals, what else is it that she had been trying *not* to hate? Is it that she wasn't able to ask him if he had been aware of her presence during all the weeks that he slept?

ELIJAH, MAN OF THE STREET

The steps from the Bethesda Fountain to the 72nd Street crossway in Central Park were very steep but Joanna had to climb them. She was walking from The Boathouse Restaurant having had one too many martinis. It was late. It was dark. No one was around because it was a winter night in February. Suddenly she lost her footing and slumped down upon the steps in slow motion as if that's what she had intended. Unable to get up on her own she sat looking up at the vast sky, enjoying the cool breeze. Then from nowhere arms appeared, picking her up, carrying her to the top of the steps where she was gently put back on her feet. They had been magical arms not connected to a body, a head, a person. Now in front of her stood a tall gaunt dark man in dark clothes, wearing a black cap. "I'm Elijah. Let me walk you out of the park." They walked in silence at first, side by side. Then he asked, "Where is that nice gentleman I always see you with?"

"My husband!" Joanna exclaimed surprised, coming out of her stupor. "He died just the other day."

As they approached the long row of benches near Central Park West, an avenue full of bright lights, he disappeared into the shadows of an arbor just past Strawberry Fields. He must live in the park, she thought.

One late afternoon, the following weekend, still in a befuddled, anguished state, she returned to Strawberry Fields and sat on one of the benches surrounding John Lennon's Memorial. Nearby a man with a guitar was singing a Beatles' song, *Eleanor Rigby* in a soulful voice. She looked all around hoping to see Elijah. But how would she recognize him? She hadn't seen his face, and even if she had she wouldn't have remembered it. She got up and walked behind the benches into a lawn area that was enclosed by tall old trees. She sat on a boulder and closed her eyes. "Hello there, señora, we meet again!" Opening her eyes she saw the gaunt man. She saw he had a full beard but his cap hid his eyes. His clothes were all black. He had long fingers with clean fingernails.

"Elijah! How good to see you! You ran off before I could thank you."

"It's okay. Do you want to take a walk with me?"

Joanna hesitated but only for a second. Taking her elbow he helped her off the boulder. As they walked down a steep hill he again held her by the elbow providing a subtle brake. Once upon the westerly circular road, they headed north on the sidewalk, drawn by glimpses of the lake through the trees.

"Elijah, where do you live?"

"Here, there, nowhere, sometimes with friends, but I always return to this place. It's mine. I belong here."

"Surely you haven't always lived like this, have you?"

"No. I've studied. I've worked. I've traveled but this is home."

"Why?"

"It's the closest thing to my homeland Puerto Rico, the gardens, ponds, waterfalls, woods, the music when the weather is good, the gourds, maracas, bongos. The Dakota, you know the big apartment building even reminds me of *El Moro*. I can imagine it having dungeons, vaults, lookouts."

"Why not go back then?"

Turning his face away he murmured, "I can't, not ever."

She didn't know why, but that evening as soon as she returned home she looked up the name Elijah in the bible, finding him in *Kings*. He had been fed "bread and flesh" by the ravens and had drunk water from a brook, but when the brook had dried up he'd been sustained by a "widow woman." In the end he'd been torn asunder by a chariot of fire and escorted into the heavens by a whirlwind. Joanna shivered, once again feeling the presence of death.

They continued to meet on a bench around Strawberry Fields every Sunday late afternoon. She found out he had been briefly married twice and had a daughter whose whereabouts he didn't know and that she'd now be in her late teens. He'd won a scholarship to a medical school but lost it to bad company and drugs. He'd been in prison for attempting to stab a policeman who was apprehending him from behind in plainclothes.

As they came to know each other better he began to take longer and longer strides, seemingly forgetting she would have trouble keeping up. She was much older than he, perhaps by twenty years. His walk was more of a strut, his head always held high, his nose crinkling with pleasure at all the sweetness as well as all the debris around them. He himself never smelled unclean so he must go somewhere regularly to wash up. Sometimes he had a strong metallic aroma around him. She asked him about it jokingly, saying it must be a new cologne. He laughed and told her of his days and nights in dingy hotel rooms with no windows, with only a cot in the corner with no sheets, a smudged sink nearby. "Even I sometimes crave a warm body near me. We smoke our pipes, we do our thing." Seeing her questioning face he added, "Crack!"

"Oh," she said, embarrassed because she was imagining him naked within clouds of smoke with bleary eyes, a slightly swollen belly like on a baby.

One day he asked her to do him a favor, to go to 60th Street and First Avenue, climb four flights of stairs to visit his older sister Olga to give her a message. She agreed. She was curious. He handed her a dusty sealed greeting card envelope.

Olga met her at her door as if she already knew Joanna, as if she expected her. She groaned, turned her back, asking her visitor to come in. Passing a pig-footed bathtub in the kitchen they entered the living room where she gestured for Joanna to sit. Olga's legs barely reached the linoleum floor as she sat glaring at her with tiny eyes that were sunk in a thick-skinned face. She sat very straight, her heavily harnessed breasts pointed at Joanna. "Well?" she asked.

Joanna gave her the envelope. As she opened and read the folded letter Joanna looked around the room already knowing by the peeping sounds that birds surrounded her. She looked out of the window at the looming Queensboro Bridge as she heard the finches bouncing around in their cages throwing their seeds to the floor. On the cocktail table between them was a vase of plastic flowers and a bowl of plastic miniature fruits and vegetables. She guessed that Olga was around her age, roughly twenty years older than Elijah. Her face remained stolid as she read what must have been a lengthy note. When she finished she tore it up, savagely throwing the pieces onto the floor. "Let me tell you what this *condenado* once did!"

"I'm sorry," Joanna said getting up, suddenly feeling frightened, "I don't want to know."

"You seem to be an intelligent, educated lady but you're stupid! What are you doing with that *hijo de una perra* (son of a bitch)! He seduced, no, *raped* my child—he knew better, he was fifteen!"

Joanna just stood there, but she wasn't shocked, knowing that Elijah did what he wanted when he wanted. She knew what he did in those dingy hotel rooms, sex and more sex, enhanced by the smoking of crack. One night stands. No responsibilities. Not having to lie, to deceive.

"Surely you're exaggerating—just sexy teenagers at play," Joanna remarked.

"You don't understand anything, so don't smile like those fucking smart-assed doctors!"

"I must leave!" And she headed for the door as Olga shouted at her, the finches getting louder and louder in their frenzied twittering.

"My child was only a little boy of nine! Elijah turned him into a *maricón* (a homosexual)!"

As Joanna descended the old marble steps dented on the middle edge by millions of footfalls she was perturbed. She didn't go near the park for many weeks. Finally it was Spring. With the funeral, the burial of her husband behind her, all in excruciating slow motion, she decided to return to the park. Maybe Elijah would be gone by now, but she knew he'd be there. She went to a promontory off 77th Street, to a little peninsula full of boulders, perfect for sitting on, for looking southwards over the entire lake watching the frogs, ducks, herons and then following the rowboats as they disappeared around the bend of the lake heading for Bethesda Fountain where she'd first met Elijah in the dead of a winter's night.

In time a voice whispered in her ear, "You look far away, angry. I gather Olga told you what you wanted to know, the reason I can't return to Puerto Rico, the reason I can't return to my family."

"Yes," she answered. They were silent for a long time. They listened intently to the water lapping against the rocks. "You've never really loved a woman have you?" She finally asked.

"I haven't loved anybody. It's hard for me to be close. Even when I'm living with someone I'm alone. I like it that way."

"So you prefer your sordid affairs in those tawdry rooms?" She asked accusingly.

"Maybe!"

Unexpectedly she turned towards him punching him hard on his upper arm, "But you enjoy being a tease, a seducer—you're a whore aren't you?"

"What's with you? Do you want me to fuck you is that it?" he asked grabbing her by her shoulders and pulling her close to him, "I could do it right here! Is that what you want? And I'll do it for nothing!"

"No, of course not!" she answered alarmed, pulling herself away from him.

After a short silence, in a low but earnest voice Elijah said, "Look, don't worry. I won't hurt you. You just made me angry with your hypocrisy, your self-righteousness."

I'm sorry," she murmured softly, patting his arm where she had hit him.

"Look, I can get turned on easily enough by just about anyone out on the streets but I can't feel more than sexual passion. Not that I want to anyway. Somewhere deep inside I know what love is but I can't really feel it. Sex and drugs makes me feel good, makes me feel safe even when I'm not, makes me not care what's happening. Sex and drugs can be dangerous but they never betray me the way humans do."

Joanna nodded, somehow knowing what he was talking about. He continued, "Even when I'm looking for another person to be with, they have to be familiar, knowable, a mirror image of myself," and he removed his cap, removed her dark glasses and looked at her straight in the eye. She saw his black, black eyes with little shiny spots within, tiny mirrors. She saw nothing reflected within them, unless, maybe, way off in the distance there was a woman who was no longer young, a person with a deep yearning in her eyes.

TRIANGLE IN BERMUDA

Joanna sat huddled in an over-soft love seat into which she sank deeper and deeper as time passed. She knew she was dreaming but she couldn't awaken herself. Windows were boarded up. Dim lights flickered in two small metal lamps adorned by painted red roses half scraped off, dripping faucets in the kitchen and in the bathroom. Who was she? The mirror described her as big, aging, dressed in black with short hair sticking up on end, aggrieved, corners of the mouth turned downward; but she felt thin, emaciated, scared. She couldn't go into the bedroom because of what was hanging over the doorway—a giant yellow fern looking like a demon spider. What was her name? Where was her handbag, her identification? In the closet hung a leather jacket with a frayed lining, two black silk trousers, two black silk shirts, and hanging separately, a long beaded necklace with a leather pouch pendant. Inside the pouch was a key that had had a gold head soldered on with tiny letters decorating it—perhaps they were words but she couldn't decipher them. No wallet. No identification.

Suddenly she awakened dismayed she wasn't in her New York City apartment. Instead she was in a hotel room in Bermuda gazing at the ocean through the open terrace door- dry mouth, gritty eyes, brittle bones, the coldest of feet that even the tropical breeze couldn't warm. Today she had to go to the hospital to see if Elijah (the new man in her life) was dead or alive after his moped accident. Upon hearing of the accident she had rushed to the Emergency Room but during the night after she'd left he'd taken a turn for the worse, one lung collapsed, the other stabbed by broken ribs—he had been placed on a ventilator.

Though she didn't feel like eating breakfast she reached into the small refrigerator for her leftover dinner of chicken and vegetables. As she poked at the food she idly looked into the dresser mirror. So, who was she? An ancient child with spiky hair looked back at her mouthing the accusatory words, "You don't see me, *me!*" But these weren't her words, they were the last words Elijah had shouted at her before leaving for his moped ride.

Throwing the mauled food into the garbage, quickly dressing, plunking a silk knitted hat on her head, she walked out into the garden; green lizards scampered away across the verdant lawn thinking they could hide among the white, yellow and red hibiscus. Continuing down the long winding path lined by lordly palm trees, she headed for the bus stop on the main road oblivious of people or cars. The glass of the bus window was so clean it reflected the scenery from the opposite side of the road—cliffs collided with ocean waves, columns of marching trees wafted up to the heavens. Elijah's face obliterated the scene, his pony-tail unfurled; gone was the look of an audacious pirate; all that remained was the hurt of the eclipsed, the unseen. "You're turning me into someone else, someone I'm not! You don't see *me!*" Elijah's words continuing to echo in her head.

She realized she'd heard similar words before, from James, her late husband after her father died, "Look at me!" he'd exclaimed. "I'm right here, alive, why are your eyes seeking the man who abandoned you, your own father, who's now gone forever?"

Lover, husband converging upon her, accusing her of a monstrous blindness, the worse of deceitfulness.

She began to wonder how the accident happened. The constable said that no other vehicle had been involved, that the moped had not hit a wall or a boulder, that it must have tipped over at a great speed. Could Elijah have just let go, closed his eyes and left the rest to fate?

She stood next to the open curtains in the Intensive Care Unit looking at Elijah in disbelief. He was not the indignant man who'd stalked out of the hotel room, not even the man she'd seen in the Emergency Room howling in pain, his arms feebly reaching out to her—now he was a giant inert baby. He was whitish gray, all swarthiness gone, mouth open with a tube stuck inside, cords connected to a machine attached to his arms and chest, naked but for a towel across his genitals. There was a soft beeping sound all around. As big as he was, as muscular, there was a gracefulness about the upward turn of his neck, a delicacy about the knees kept apart by a pillow, knees bruised as if from kneeling in worship for a long time. As hard as she tried she couldn't help but see him, feel him as a mirage, as a being from long ago. She tore off her hat, her hair springing up in all directions like a nest of vipers or a melting halo. The insistent beeping sound was like a communication from Elijah. What was he saying? What was he saying to her that he hadn't said earlier? What had her life been saying to her all along?

She knew the answer was in her dream, in the words written upon the golden key, the words she had not been able to decipher.

Cloak and Dagger

The barricades were up. It was a special preview at the Museum of Modern Art in New York City and a large crowd was expected. Joanna was meeting a friend at the entrance since they were coming from opposite sides of the city, he from the east of Central Park and she from the west of the park. Arriving a few minutes earlier she was able to straighten out her garments—a long scarf had gotten twisted, tightening itself around her neck making her feel a little strangled. After catching her breath she began to look up and down the street for a sign of Kyle. She looked forward to seeing him but this was not a date; he was the husband of an old friend who was out-of-town on a long extended business trip. It was a balmy night in October. People were arriving in fancy garb not hidden by overcoats—women in frilly miniskirts, glittering tiny camisoles and pointed-toe stiletto-heels—men in bright-colored jackets with no collars or lapels. She liked this minimalist look though she still missed puffy ball gowns, flowing cocktail dresses and classical tuxedo jackets. It used to be such fun years and years ago to saunter through the streets with her late husband James, she with a long satin dress hiding her walking shoes and he in a striped jacket, beret and red espadrilles. Kyle and his wife Viveca often joined them in their dressing-up and walking for miles to a restaurant, concert or art exhibit. She and James hardly ever had an event in their home that wasn't a costume party, always with a theme, 'famous lovers in literature' and sometimes even 'nightmare apparitions.'

Now as she waited, all in ample black but not from mourning since James had been dead for several years, she began to worry.

Kyle was nowhere in sight; she'd been waiting over a half hour. It was not like him to be late for their get-togethers. Deep down she'd had a foreboding that he would not show up. What is it that had transpired the last time they had seen each other? He had commented on one of her short-stories, "I'm intrigued by what is true and what isn't."

"What is it you want to know?" She had queried, surprised at how serious he looked, at how he'd tousled his thinning black hair on top of his head by running his long fingers roughly through it. It was not like him. He had always been calm and composed, never tempestuous like her James.

"Well, I'm not sure but in *Eros in the Doll Corner* for instance— was the real Pépe in your life a sexy little rascal or did you just create him that way?"

"I don't understand."

"Is it possible that Pépe was in reality just a nice passive boy whom you transformed to suit yourself, as a writer of course, or is it that the girl in your story had the capability to bring out in Pépe a side of him that had been totally buried?"

She couldn't remember what she had answered, probably because she had dodged the question in some way, feeling uncomfortable, criticized. Now, standing there in the street with excited voices assailing her from all sides, she wondered if he was thinking that she was imagining him to be other than who he was?

Perturbed, now certain Kyle would not show up, she entered the museum, heading for the nearest bar, ordering a Jack Daniels on the rocks, drinking it all down in one swallow hardly aware of all the faces and bodies swirling around her. Then taking several escalators up to one of the top floors she began to look for her favorite paintings, David Alfaro Siqueiros' fiery *Collective Suicide* and his *Echo of a Scream* depicting a large baby in agony. Despite the drink which normally would have relaxed her, she felt stiffly coiled up inside. She tried chuckling at Egon Schiele's women exposing themselves without shame but only a raking burp came out. As she looked at René Magrittes' giant *Eye*, she suddenly felt as if she were being spied on. She turned around as quickly as her chronic vertigo would permit but saw only a collage of long graceful legs and dazzling smiles. No one was looking in her direction. Even the waiters with their trays of goodies held high by-passed her as they headed for vivacious clusters of young life. Why did she imagine what wasn't there or did she? Was it a bad thing? But all this wasn't what was disturbing her. "Okay," she murmured softly to herself, "Face it, you've been stood up and you hate it! Oh fuck it, it's more than that, way more than that, way more than Kyle himself, you're deeply, deeply hurt, disappointed, crushed with feelings of an absolute rejection, a global abstraction of pure abandonment!"

She stood at the edge of the atrium, bending over the railing, looking down all the way to the ground floor, hoping to see Kyle looking for her, but only the inchoate mixture of laughter and words swept up to her. As she continued into the next gallery full of Pablo Picasso's nude women freely romping on the beach without self-consciousness the feeling of being watched persisted. It was as if someone were stalking her, as if someone wanted to catch her, to uncloak and unmask her, to render her naked in body and soul, a large shivering mass of collapsing muscle and rippled skin, a being scared to death of aloneness.

Shaking all over she went into the nearest bathroom—empty, shiny, pristine. All the gaiety was shut out. As her urinal tinkle resounded pitifully, she heard the door open. She followed the flat-shoed footsteps to the washbasin where the faucet was turned on. Someone must be looking into the mirror as hair was patted into place by water. But in time the out-pouring became heavier and heavier, louder and louder. The water had to be splashing everywhere in sight, she thought to herself. Very soon as she sat in her stall, her pants and underwear still lowered, she began to feel as if the spurts of water were coming in her direction, almost reaching her head, warming and soothing the top of it. Then the faucet was abruptly turned off. She waited for the footsteps to resume but all was quiet. She waited even longer but not a sound. Eventually she stood up, arranged her clothing and cautiously opened the door. No one was there. No one at all.

Perplexed but now totally calm she began to wander once again, no longer feeling spied on but also no longer feeling alone. At last she was able to truly laugh as she realized that she felt as if she had been patted on the head, as if she had received a blessing of sorts from an invisible hand.

HOUND ON THE HUNT

What was it about Central Park that drew Joanna there over and over again? Ancient trees and boulders. They made her wonder what spirits, what secrets they held within, especially in the early evenings when the diminishing light created an atmosphere of a waking dream, a conscious sleep, a fugue state, perhaps even the atmosphere of a life in death, an afterlife.

As a chill reached over her very bones, though it was a warm October evening with a balmy breeze, she asked herself if she shouldn't be worried about possible lurking dangers. But then it wasn't that late, far from midnight and she was on a well-traveled route crossing the park on a thoroughfare from West to East. People were jogging, walking dogs, cuddling with their partners as they strolled. However, imperceptibly it became dark. Her heart beat a little faster, her temples throbbed, the adrenaline loosening her stiff limbs a little. Why should she now be worried about danger? What could be more dangerous than being in love and she had been in love most of her life.

As she walked on she told herself that at least she would be spared the anxiety of running away from whoever was chasing her, a mugger or any other culprit, since there was no way she could ever run again, not with her artificial knees, her feet with their bone implants, a neck held together by wire and glue. Ironically, she would have the luxury of having no other option but turning to face her pursuer, to confront. She would be spared the torment of Francis Thompson who in his poem *The Hound of Heaven* wrote "I fled him down the nights and down the days; I fled him down the arches of the years; I fled him down the labyrinthine ways of my own mind and in the midst of tears I hid from him…From those strong feet that followed."

Once again she realized that she had never turned to face the love of her life, now gone forever, disappearing into another's arms, the arms of death. It hardly mattered who he was, only that he had been. But was it a "he," her father or her husband of many years, or was it a "she," her mother, her first love?

Arriving at the grand staircase leading down to the Bethesda Fountain, she leaned her elbows on the balustrade. It felt good to press her belly on the stone. She lost track of time, of the hour, the day, even of the year itself. All she knew was that she wasn't old anymore, nor young, nor somewhere in between. She just was.

Slowly out of the mistiness of the moment, she sensed a presence, not behind her but by her side—small, quiet, hardly breathing. Keeping one hand on the cement wall she straightened up and turned around. Her mother was looking at her—how tiny she was, barely up to Joanna's shoulders. She looked at her mother closely perhaps in a way she never had before, having mainly felt her fluffiness, smelled her dewy fresh sweat, endured her fingers reaching for her, pulling her back. Most of the time she hadn't seen her mother at all. Now Joanna saw that her eyes were like semi-precious stones, like dark tiger-eyes. What was it she saw within the streaks of black and gold? Sadness, yes. Questioning, yes. Pride, no. Recognition, yes and no. Doubt, regret, yes, yes, yes. Joanna wanted to banish that look. She bent over to embrace her, to kiss her *mejillas*, her silky round prominent cheekbones. She kissed her soft full lips at the corners trying to uplift their downward slope. Her lips felt smooth like the satins she had always worn across her body, her breasts, the satins of her nightgowns, her dressing gowns, blouses and evening dresses, always in shades of pinks, blues, highlighting her olive-shaded skin.

"Mama, how wonderful to see you!"

"Mi hija, mi hijita, que bueno verte!"

Joanna reached for her hands, holding them tightly, "It's been so long. You've been so far away. There's so much I need to ask you. How much time do we have?"

"Not long," she answered, wincing a little at Joanna's hold on her hands.

"Quick, quick," Joanna whispered to herself, "spill it out, ask what you want, do it once and for all!" But her mind went blank. She had become "*atarantada*," as if poisoned by a tarantula which had sent her into a frenzied dance without words.

The mother gently pried her hands free, "You wanted to talk to me, *mi hija*, what about? Tell me. You so seldom wanted to talk to me or ask me anything as if I would not hear you or understand or know the answer.

"I always thought you disliked me," Joanna was barely audible.

"Why did you think that?" she answered with no hint of surprise or even of denial.

"It was the way you looked at me as if I'd done something bad, something really bad that made you disgusted with me."

Taking her by the elbow the mother led her down the stairs to the benches surrounding the waterless fountain, baby-stepping along with her daughter. They sat sideways so they could face each other. "You're right," the mother began, "there was something wrong between us from the very beginning, from before you were born."

Joanna leaned one of her elbows on the back of the bench and crossed her legs as Benita continued, "I know you've known for a long time that I was married once before, before I even met your father, but what your father never wanted you to know was that when we met I was his housekeeper and cook, a maid really, and my husband cleaned out the hangers at the airport that your papa managed."

Joanna frowned.

"Your father and I fell in love, well, not really. He may have, but I didn't. I wanted to fall in love but I couldn't. However, I liked him and he pursued me with such hunger. I was flattered though his neediness frightened me sometimes. As you've always known he had suffered a great deal ever since he was a little boy, love somehow always eluding him, but no matter what he was still *el gran Americano, el gran hombre, el Jéfe* and I was only a twenty year old half-Maya woman full of shame. Before long I felt even more crushed by shame when I became pregnant with you and I didn't know who the father was. You see my husband took me whenever it pleased him, even when I said "no."

"What?" I exclaimed.

"No, don't worry, it turned out to be your papa—you look so much like him." After a short pause she continued, "When it was obvious I was with child your father got a transfer from Mexico to Central America and, before he even knew that you were his, he persuaded me to elope with him. I was overjoyed. I thought that at last I'd found a man who would not judge me, condemn me, a man who would love me as a woman who was not just a *culo*, no better than a female goat or sheep."

Benita went on to describe how she and Keith ended up on an isolated, desolate peninsula where he was to create a small airport for seaplanes. She came to realize that he did not trust her, that he wanted her all to himself and that once again she was, in effect, a captive. When Joanna's birth was imminent he insisted on being the one to bring her into the world with the assistance of a midwife. He needed to be the first to see if the baby resembled him or the "other." "After he bathed you," Benita said, "seeing your creamy white skin, your round hazel eyes, your delicate mouth and, above all, your dimples, he trotted around the room with you clutched so tightly against his chest that you couldn't even cry the natural cry of a baby. As he cried out with joy it was as if only he could utter the *grito* of a newborn. And that was the beginning of the real divide between you and me."

"But didn't you fight to get me back?"

"Oh yes, I kept you in my bed for a whole year, breastfeeding you anytime you wanted, imbuing you with my *leche pura*, my very own substance. But one day, my nipples became red and swollen. I felt an excruciating pain not only in my breasts but deep inside my whole being. In addition, your father was beginning to hound me, wanting me to return to his bed—he had once even insisted on drinking from my breast."

"My God!" Joanna exclaimed softly.

"Anyway, feeling totally drained I tossed you into your crib in the next room. I shoved a bottle into your greedy mouth. You screamed and thrashed around throwing that first bottle and all subsequent bottles onto the floor with a *genio* I hadn't seen in you earlier. I began to hate what I saw as the arrogance of the small, the pitiful, the helpless. I even hated you." Laughing a little while patting the side of Joanna's face, Benita continued, "I knew your *mala leche*, irritable temperament could not sustain you so I began to give you warm milk in a cup. At first you pushed it violently away, spilling it all over yourself but still licking up the drops that had fallen near your mouth, until one day you eagerly grabbed the cup and drank from it, your big eyes fixed on me."

Benita's face then became stern, "Very soon after that you became impossible to control, climbing out of your crib when no one was looking and creeping all over the house, hiding in closets, under furniture, blending in with clothing, with the laundry in the laundry room, with the urns in the kitchen. Other times you scurried very fast like a lizard, a chameleon, grinning your grin of two tiny sharp teeth."

Sitting on the bench looking at the mother, Joanna was overcome by such an immense feeling of contrariness that she began to laugh uncontrollably. Benita didn't smile. Joanna laughed even more. Benita blinked wildly, "And once you began to walk we had to be with you every minute or you'd be out the door, down the pier and into a rowboat or into the sea."

Trying to stifle her laughter Joanna put a consoling hand on

Benita's shoulder. The hand was shrugged off, "It was around that time that you began to mock me, to disobey me, to run away from me, screaming that I wasn't your mother." She paused, taking a deep breath, "And so when you were four I let your father take you over."

Joanna's mirth left her as she remembered, being forced to take a boat trip alone with her father all the way to New York so he could show her off to his previously estranged mother. She had thrown up and cried almost all the way there and back. She hated her grandmother's pasty white face, her beady blue eyes with no lashes, her sharp nose, her aroma of dry scouring powder. She missed her mother's soft features, her silky swarthiness. Then on one of their last days on the way back she stopped crying; Keith had taken her into the shower with him, probably to clean her up as well as to distract her. He lifted her high, up to the showerhead, over and over, while she screeched happily; she loved swooping through space feeling the power of flowing water and of strong arms. But what she had never been able to remember is why her mood changed so drastically by the time she saw Benita on the dock. She recalled sauntering towards her, carrying a large sack of gifts, toys from New York; she had handed the bag to her mother saying, "This belongs to you, not to me."

As if reading Joanna's mind that evening in the park as they stared at the dry fountain, Benita murmured, "You changed completely after that trip. You stopped running around like a *loca*; you didn't even answer me back. You became serious, pensive. My heart softened towards you. You began to remind me of myself when I was a child."

They both sat quietly, not saying anything for a long time. Then Joanna asked, she finally asked what she had wanted to ask from the very beginning, "Remember long ago when papa died and I fell apart and began seeing a psychiatrist and you insisted on going with me—you said there was something he needed to know?"

"Yes, I remember."

"But when he refused to see you without my being present, you backed out. Why? What was it you didn't want me to hear? To know? I never had the nerve to ask you."

Benita lowered her eyes as tears fell upon her cheeks. Even her shoulders drooped, her belly becoming distended, looking too large for her slender legs and tiny feet. Joanna grabbed her, holding her roughly, kissing the top of her silver streaked black hair, undoing her upsweep so that long strands of hair began to cascade down upon her wet face. Benita whispered, "Even now I can't tell you."

"Why not? It didn't kill me, whatever it was; I've lived a life, a long life."

"But it did kill you, in a way."

Joanna let go of her, "What do you mean?"

"Before that trip you had been a terror, a *malcriada terible* but you were all there to be seen, heard and felt. After the trip you became a shadow, a ghost. You became someone else." She looked at me intently, "Tell me, what did *you* think I wanted to tell your doctor?"

Joanna sighed, "Something about my relationship with papa, maybe we'd always been too close for your liking, maybe you were jealous and that's why you disliked me."

"No, no. I wanted to tell your doctor that I was the one who made you sick in mind and in body. Not purposely. But I caused you to get your awful disease when you were still so young. I didn't wish it upon you but I gave you all your pain, leading to all your deformities, your difficulties in movement."

Scowling Joanna backed away as Benita continued talking between sobs that made her body tremble, "In some kind of uncanny way I used you to stage a repeat of my childhood, my girlhood of maltreatment at the hands of adults, adult men."

"But why? Why didn't you protect me even more?"

"I don't know. I don't know. All I know is that I hated myself so much. Perhaps I needed to hate you too so I wouldn't envy you. Perhaps I needed to disable you the way my spirit had been disabled so we would be the same, so we could be soul mates, not one better than the other, not one superior to the other."

Joanna shook her head, "Mama, you can't cause another person to get a disease like rheumatoid arthritis—it's a complicated illness; there are many diverse factors involved." Taking a very deep breath she continued, "Otherwise, have you considered that I myself could have caused my own disease so that *you* didn't need to envy me or to fear me?"

Benita's tiger-eyes opened wide as she stared at her daughter, perplexed. They sat for a long time looking into each other's eyes. Then almost at the same moment they stood up reaching for each other's elbows, both chuckling. It was late. It was time to part. Instead of the stairs they took the winding path up to the street, to the sidewalk where they would now head westward. They walked arm-in-arm, slowly, in step with each other, despite the small feet of one and the large feet of the other.

THE CLAW AND THE CLOVEN HOOF

As Joanna approached the restaurant she tensed her muscles—there were three steps to be climbed. Bending forward as she reached for the wall she resisted seeing herself as a creature on all fours. She must concentrate on the flow of her silk kimono jacket and the glow of the deep red amber beads around her neck.

Halfway up the steps a young waiter emerged from behind the red velvet drapes to lend a hand. Edwin was already waiting in a corner booth. He was early. Now she wouldn't have time to fix her hair; it had probably parted on top to form two curving waves, something like horns. As she sat down she noticed that Edwin already had an open bottle of Cabernet Sauvignon and two goblets waiting on the table. She would have preferred to start with a gin martini but she decided she could do without. He seemed considerably older, grayer, balder than he'd looked on their first date a few weeks before. What a pair they made—he was all angles, pointed elbows, boney square shoulders, a triangular face and she was all concentric circles. His maimed hand sat right there on top of the tablecloth, five fingers fused into two prongs, whereas her deformities were mainly out of sight beneath long sleeves and slacks. She'd assumed the first time they'd met that he had sustained a war injury. Come to think of it hers were also the result of a war, an inner one, cells warring with each other leaving behind inflamed and twisted joints.

As each of them disappeared behind their giant leatherbound menus, Joanna wondered if she'd be able to say what she desperately needed to say. Then without hesitating any further she blurted out, "I was very disconcerted by your behavior the last time we met, your running out on me at the end." The truth was she'd been devastated, feeling belittled, diminished, rejected and abandoned.

"I don't know what you're talking about," he mumbled softly, smiling in an infinitely patient way as if to say, "Surely I didn't do any such thing!"

"Remember? You rushed to the bathroom at the pub and upon returning as you plunked down some money on the bar you announced you had to leave." Edwin's small sunken-in eyes widened as she continued, "I thought that perhaps you'd received an emergency call on your cell."

Edwin sighed with relief, "Well maybe that's it. I don't recall exactly but it might have been around the time my daughter needed me."

"In any case you insisted on walking me to the next corner. That was nice but then you rushed ahead leaving me trailing behind even after I asked you to slow down, even after I told you that I couldn't walk fast because of a bad ankle and foot."

"I honestly don't remember!" Then after a moment he added, "Shall we get back to the menu—I'm starved!"

Joanna glanced once again at the menus' manifold pages; too many choices; it was hard to concentrate. "Okay, if you don't remember there's nothing we can do about it." Liar, liar! What's the matter with you? she thought. What do you have to lose, why not press for an adequate response from him? But what would that be? Perhaps there was none. Perhaps the problem was all in her head.

Edwin closed his menu as if he'd already decided what he wanted to order, "Look, I'm sorry, I really am. Even though I don't remember I hate the idea that I was so rude. Please forgive me. It certainly wasn't intentional."

Nodding in acceptance of his words Joanna declared, "Well I know what I'm having, two appetizers—oysters on the half shell and steamed mussels." .

"Sounds so meager!" he mocked affectionately, "Let's share a roast rack of lamb, a kind of offering to atone for my maldeeds!"

Joanna laughed, "Yes let's do that, nice and bloody, but I still want my oysters and mussels. After all we all began as creatures from the sea and parts of our bodies still look as if they belong at the bottom of the darkest deepest ocean!" They both laughed heartily.

After placing their orders and refilling their goblets, Edwin leaned back on the banquette, "You're a very strange woman but I like you, I really do. Tell me what your love life has been like since your husband died?"

"I don't know if I want—" Joanna began.

"Okay, okay, I'll go first. I'll tell you what I've been up to since *my* wife died."

Joanna nodded in agreement trying not to grimace; one of her ankles ached; she could feel it bloating up, throbbing.

Her oysters and his escargots arrived as Edwin began, "Thank God for modern technology, the Internet—what a way to gather information, to obtain knowledge of all the people out there looking for one another!"

"That's how you meet women?"

"You sound doubtful! Why not get together with women who know and advertise what they want and are ready to go for it?"

"It sounds so crude, so mechanical!"

"Well I'm also a good friend to many widows, you know wives of old buddies of mine! Do you like that better?"

Their plates were now full of empty shells. "You mean you service them like a bull services a herd of cows?"

"Now who's being crass?" Edwin chuckled wiping off the shiny ring around his lips.

"Sorry!" Joanna laughed, "so did you find a woman who suited you through the Internet?"

"Oh yes, one in particular but it was just my luck to have

fallen for a divorcée who wasn't really ready to look at her sexual needs in an honest way. Drove me wild!"

"What do you mean?"

"You really want to know?" he queried smiling in a knowing way.

"Yes." Joanna was puzzled.

"Some women prefer to solace themselves rather than start over again with a new man."

Joanna blinked. They stopped talking as her mussels and his salad with a gorgonzola dressing were placed in front of them. She asked, "What makes you think they want or need sex?"

"Oh come on now, *everybody* wants it no matter their age or state of health but it doesn't have to be copulation; it can be touching, patting, kissing and all of their variations.

"Maybe you're right," Joanna began digging the little fork in between the partially opened mussel shells and bringing the dark morsels up to her mouth, "but isn't it possible to sublimate this need, to find it in a love affair with ideas, symbols? Or how about finding it in a passionate connection with a kind of collective other?"

Edwin stopped eating, "You're getting stranger and stranger, I love it, you're such a mystery!" Then as he went back to finishing his salad he added, "However you're forgetting that we're made up of both body and spirit, there's no way around it, you can't just shove the body into oblivion!"

Seeing that their bottle was empty Edwin motioned to the waiter to bring another. "You're not going to get away with it you know!" Edwin's voice was louder than usual.

"What are you talking about?" Joanna stammered.

"Don't look so alarmed," Edwin laughed. "You're not going to get away with hiding out in your world of abstractions because it's now *your* turn to tell what you've been doing about love since your husband died!"

Sighing, drinking from the new bottle, Joanna said, "Well, I had a lover, younger than I but middle-aged, a man looking for love after a lifetime of easy-come, easy-go sex!"

"So, you provided the love, what did *you* get? I gather it's over now, no?"

"It wasn't meant to last but for awhile we completed each other."

"You're so coyly indirect. Was it good sex, you know fulfilling?"

"Of course."

"Why don't I believe you?"

Joanna laughed, "You can't imagine a romantic like me being able to give myself up to the physical, the erotic, right?"

"That's right!"

"It's *because* of my romanticism, my metaphoric style of living that I can get off even with damaged, wounded men."

"Oh, ohhh, how intriguing, tell me more!"

At that moment the rack of lamb arrived already separated into two platters of gleaming meat surrounded by tiny potatoes and string beans. Joanna took a long gulp of her wine and then after cutting up her meat into small pieces she continued, "You talked of opposites before; I'm reminded of Anatole Frances' *Thaïs* where, because of their great love for each other, the priest and the whore end up resembling each other, he a dissipated man and she a saint."

"What's your point?"

"That imagination can be transforming!"

"I still don't see what you're getting at!"

"I'm not sure either, maybe I've had too much wine! Maybe the Thaïs thing isn't a good example. Well, take Duc Jean des Esseintes in Huysman's novel *Against the Grain*."

"In the end Jean found the greatest of joy, of pleasure, a fulfilling salvation in the drinking of the water with which he had washed the bodies of lepers!"

Edwin put down his utensils, laughing raucously, "Wow! You

certainly are high-minded! But tell me, when you say you get off even with damaged men do you mean it metaphorically or do you get a real earthly orgasm?"

Joanna only smiled at him as if to say, "Wouldn't you like to know?"

"I knew you weren't going to answer me," he chuckled.

They were silent for a long time, not making a sound not even the sound of chewing, of breathing, of swallowing. Finally, pushing his empty plate away, Edwin said softly, "You know you're a flirt, a tease, a femme fatale of the highest order! But, of course, you know that, don't you, you've cultivated that image, haven't you?"

At first Joanna said nothing as she too pushed her plate away abandoning its few remaining shreds of lamb. She was deeply perturbed. His words had rung the proverbial bell in her mind, in her memory: her father training her to be a woman of the world; her first husband's father saying in a severe voice that her answers were "always short of being ingenuous;" her late husband, her second husband, forever questioning the reality of her love for him; all labeling her, branding her, making her their own.

Finally she responded, "No, you're wrong but it doesn't matter. You and I wouldn't make a good couple anyway."

Edwin reached across the table with both of his hands, the good one and the deformed one and put both her hands with all of their swollen joints in between. "There you are totally wrong, we are perfectly suited for each other. I find you very exciting."

Gently Joanna pulled her hands away but kept them close to his. She ached from head to toe. Something was very wrong. She felt trapped as if she couldn't move on her own, as if she couldn't breathe on her own, as if she'd fall by the wayside if she didn't remain by the side of the other. Suddenly she knew why she'd felt so devastated by Edwin's rapid stride down the street, by her humiliating efforts to keep up. At that moment she'd realized, without knowing it, that she was reliving, reenacting an old scenario. All the important men in her life had needed her to walk at their stride. They had needed her to mirror them, to complete their tattered selves. Because she wanted to be loved she had struggled to keep up, to remain by their side, no matter how difficult, no matter what harm it caused her.

Though still transfixed in place, looking merely thoughtful, tranquil—in her mind Joanna could hear herself screaming, sobbing out loud, trashing around on the floor, on all fours without caring how she looked or sounded. Oddly enough at the same moment she knew that at the end of the evening Edwin would walk her home, that he'd take her arm and walk at her pace. But she also knew that when they reached her doorway she'd say goodnight and goodbye. Yes, he was right. They could make a perfect couple, *too* perfect.

DOWN TO EARTH

As Joanna entered her apartment and turned on the light, the music box which only worked when a radiance surrounded it, began its usual song. However, the tune was gone. Only a squeak remained. Soon it would be time to throw it out. After all, it was only an inexpensive novelty that had come in a package with a bottle of liquor. For several years, every time it sang out she had said either "Good morning, dear man" or "Good evening, dear man." As she stood at the washbasin brushing her teeth she thought she should say "Goodbye, dear one," but she couldn't, not yet.

She had already removed her jewelry, undressed, emptied her handbag and put everything away in its place. Even her mail had been sorted. She stood only in her underpants looking into the mirror grateful it only revealed her head and shoulders. Suddenly very tired she turned away abruptly eager to get to bed, to sleep. The next thing she knew she was sitting on the floor dazed but knowing that she wouldn't be able to get up on her own. But she wasn't alarmed as if she belonged there on the ground. Everything looked different all around her; she had descended into another world. Could it be she was already asleep, dreaming? Scooting along on her behind she moved out of the bathroom her legs wriggling, her hands pushing against the wooden floor like bent flippers, an ape's humped torso, a Chimera of sorts. Within a confusion, working hard to focus she saw the golden face of King Agamemnon, a copy of his death mask on a bottom shelf in the hallway, his closed eyelids flickering, high cheekbones bursting through his skin, fine lips pouting, goatee pointing at her. He resembled her late husband's face as he lay dying in their king-sized bed, in their yellow bedroom almost ten years ago. It was morning when he died. They had listened to Vivaldi's *Double Concerto* over and over again all night long, lying side-by-side wedged against each other. She had longed to envelop his head in a giant embrace, to kiss his cheeks, chew on his lips but he was totally engrossed elsewhere, weakly shrugging her off. "I want to feel every last second; I want to know what it is to die," he had said to her days before. As the end approached they were not together not like the first time they danced improvising to the Latin music at El Morocco Nightclub, alternately following each other's lead as if well-rehearsed, limbs and muscles blending, faces incandescent with the pleasure of being one with another.

Slithering onward into the living room still not wondering how she was to get up, she came face-to-face with her life-size papier-mâché jaguar created by one of her sisters to celebrate their Mexican heritage—vivid green cat's eyes, blasé, confident, no thought except to do what was natural with no guilt, regret, doubts, with no choices to make, just to be, to do, to exist. The jaguar had nothing to say to her, nor she to it except "You're beautiful!"

Joanna humped, pumped along to the cocktail table where there lay a tray of ivory Netsukes and other small statues. Resting her elbows on the edge of the table she looked at them carefully looking for something: *The Three Monkeys*, don't hear, don't see, don't speak; *The Failed Nun* on her stomach, bare arse up in the air, robe around her neck and shoulders, arms and hands out of sight, mouth forming a perfect circle as in rapid breathing; *Winged Demon* emerging from an eggshell, expectant, surprised, angry; *Stunted Black Figure* with eyes wide open with fright, skinny arms wrapped around itself. Joanna rested her head on the lacquer table "What am I doing? What is the matter with me?" She answered herself, "Don't be such a coward. Lean into it all. How often in one's life does one have the opportunity to be down with the forgotten, the invisible, the escaped, the fallen?"

Looking up beyond the little creatures she saw a large form by the terrace door on the floor under a plant table dimly illuminated by the lanterns on the roof garden across the way. It was one of her mother's ceramics looking like a headless woman with enormous hips, no legs, a fertility urn. Dear little Indian mother, *una pobrecita*, not referring to the poverty of her growing up but to her fragility, vulnerability. Never showed this more than when she was dying in that antiquated castle of a hospital in England, in that enormous hall with high vaulted ceilings, twenty beds on each side but with spaciousness between each. Some patients were hidden behind closed curtains, others sat up talking to visitors, others lay quietly like corpses but with rosy cheeks. This was fifteen years ago when her mother had suffered a massive stroke, no longer moving, speaking, one infected eye patched up. "Mama I always loved you though I didn't know it. To me you were only a lowly woman, a cook, housecleaner, washerwoman, scolding nag. I had no appreciation of the fact you'd given birth to me, to my sisters, that you were my beloved father's chosen wife, lover, companion, that you were an artist!" One of Benita's hands was alive responding to Joanna's words by slightly squeezing her hand. Joanna put her head down under her mother's hand needing to feel her soft strokes upon her face. She thought she heard her cooing as her fingers lightly brushed across one ear, one eye and came to rest upon Joanna's lips. Her fingers moved no more. She died three hours later. Joanna cried for hours, days, a long time, mourning her being so squashed, vanquished, erased, so laid low.

Marveling at how well she could pivot on her behind she moved away from the windows ending up in front of her fireplace. She hadn't used it in ages much less looked at what she had stored within its blackened walls. Among the African brass statues was a large brass urn, a gold bracelet around its breast-shaped lid with a plaque that bore no name. It was hard to believe she still held on to half of him, half of her lover's ashes, the other half having been given to his family three years ago. "I must get him to Central Park as I promised!" She mumbled trying not to remember his last days when death was inevitable—half propped up, immobile, eyes popped open, fixed in an expression of terror, oxygen tubes in his nostrils, dry cracked lips, clenched fists on his thighs. "He can't possibly feel anything, not with all the morphine we keep giving him!" His doctor kept assuring her as she shook her head in a torture of disbelief. "Don't worry, he's at rest! The nurses exclaimed as they put a tube down his throat for nutrition and medication. Nevertheless finally Joanna and his doctors decided to remove all the tubes allowing him to die more quickly.

Joanna stretched out flat on the floor. Soon she began to pound on the floor with her fists, then she pushed at an invisible encasement over and around her, beating at the sides with her elbows as if she had been buried alive in a coffin. "Let me out of here! I'm still alive!" She screamed inside her head until she was tired and ready to get up, wanting and needing to get up. It seemed to her that she glided into the bedroom where she went for a pair of slacks and a top and into the kitchen for the long rod with a claw at one end called a Reacher that could be used to take the chain off her door. She looked into her address book for the phone number of her building's front desk since she couldn't reach the intercom.

The doorman, a strong young man got her up lifting her up from behind. As she stood tall on her own two feet she felt like crying not only out of an immense joyous relief such as she had seldom felt but also because she hated saying goodbye to those she knew she had to release, finally, even the one who had not appeared that night, the one who had died first, long before husband, mother, lover—her father. He was the first to go but he had not left. He was still alive. Perhaps he would even survive her. His power, the power of the undead, of the tormented ones who cannot live nor can they die, lives forever.

II.
THE LIFE OF A MAYA-AMERICAN WOMAN

STRANGER IN THE BAT CAVE

Joanna stood on the edge of the cenote, a deep wide well in Chichén-Itzá, the ancient Maya ruins in Mexico, not far from her mother's homeland in Quintana Roo. Her naked body underneath the embroidered white gown had been painted blue, leaving her skin vibrant with rippling nerves. The jade necklaces cascaded down upon her raised nipples and taut belly. Smiling contentedly as she savored the taste of the chocolate mangoes that still lingered in her mouth, she swayed a little, intoxicated by the special tea she had been given. She felt young, beautiful and privileged. As an innocent Maya maiden she was to be sacrificed to Zotz, the Maya Bat God. There were two men next to her, one on each side, both wearing feather headdresses and loin cloths full of tiny mirrors, which reflected her as a mosaic, as if she had been put together piece-by-piece by diverse magical powers. The two priests began to chant. Their words were foreign, strange, as if coming from afar. Feeling soothed, she closed her eyes, allowing her swaying movements to lead her into a serpentine dance. Suddenly she heard words in English which she did not comprehend. It was then that she knew she was dreaming and with this knowledge came the shocking realization that her husband James was dead and buried. She tried with all her burgeoning consciousness to revive the vibrancy of her flesh. She wanted to return to the delicious state of inebriation. But instead she was trapped between total wakefulness and a deep sleep, experiencing a mounting sense of horror; she was about to be killed, murdered. But what was worse was that it was James who was speaking the English words, in his New York accent,

"You never answered my question!" Joanna turned to face the voice, to face the priest who spoke. He was golden brown with fierce black eyes and full lips, so unlike James with his deep blue eyes and delicately sensuous mouth. "Why didn't you answer my question?" the raspy voice asked again.

The second priest, also brown, sang out in a sonorous voice as he coiled a vine around Joanna's ankles, "Down into the depths you must go!"

Abruptly, with a violent force, the two priests lifted her high up into the air and as she screamed, they threw her into the murky waters of the well, her gown sweeping upwards over her head and uplifted arms, ballooning out, so she looked like a blue-stemmed flower in full bloom.

Joanna awakened, crying out. She was lying on the same king-size bed in which James had died, not so long before, in the yellow bedroom, on the upper west side, in New York City. Only a couple of weeks ago, on her sixty-third birthday, when she had been bemoaning her aloneness out loud as she had lain by his side, thinking he was asleep, he had reached out, clutching her hand with his usual fervor saying, "Happy Birthday, dear pussycat!"

But as she tried to concentrate on the enduring love she and James had had for each other for nearly forty years, the dream, his angry words, constantly intruded. She couldn't fully comprehend what it was she was telling herself in the dream. She knew she was telling herself that there was a question to be answered, a mystery to be solved, the puzzle of her personality, of her whole life, to be acknowledged.

As the days passed she thought more and more about the dream and why it was she had conjured up the idea of being sacrificed to Zotz, the Maya deity, a vampire bat. Perhaps her dream had been a prelude to a Vision Quest. She had seen photographs of ancient Maya temples, depicting Zotz in anthropomorphic form, lovingly holding a bat baby. She had seen, on her frequent trips to Mexico, that there were underground caverns branching off from the bottom of cenotes, housing whole families of vampire bats. What was the light she must find within their darkness? What was the life-sustaining essence she must imbibe? A sacrifice had been made. A vision had been received. The urgency of a quest to be made had been felt.

In her mind's eye, she began to see one bat standing out from all the others. He had a nose that looked like two leaves. He was flying out of the cenote feeling impelled to leave. The waters had turned brackish, the gardens were dying. There was little to feed on. He must fly north to seek a better place. He must leave old Mexico and fly to New Mexico to find a new cave. But, above all, he was coming to meet her. She knew she must go to Bandelier State Park in New Mexico to look for the bat caves up on the mountainside.

Within a few days, she was walking on a winding path in New Mexico to the ancient dwellings of the Anazasi Indians, knowing from the map in the glove compartment of the car she had rented in Santa Fe, that the Bat Cave was on the far end of the park. Stopping to rest on a bench facing the cliffs, Joanna listened to the distant echoes of other visitors' voices. Suddenly the cliff walls began to lean down towards her, her eyelids fell over her glazed eyes. Feeling drugged, she lay down on the bench, immediately feeling the prickliness of the ants underneath her back, buttocks, legs. Deep below the bench she felt the ancient tensions within the earth, the fissures, the cracks, the eruptions of ash, gases, dust, cinders and hot lava. She thought she saw the disembodied head of her father with his enormous forehead, with his wispy tufts of hair and his violet eyes. Was he the second priest in her dream? She saw circular shapes floating around, sometimes joining together to form a voluptuous, motherly body, then roundnesses breaking off and drifting off in different directions. Who and what was she? She asked herself, as she remembered the sparkling blue mosaic reflected in the mirrors of the priests—a hybrid, hyphenated, many-genomed self that had originated with the merger of her

English-Irish father and her Mexican-Maya Indian mother, a self born in Guatemala, and thereafter traveling far and wide. Then she saw James once again but not as a priest but as a dying man, his body arching upwards, shuddering in violent spasms, as if being torn asunder by an invisible force, perhaps by his own turbulent, tormented life, his passionate longing for an absolute love that had become fixated on Joanna, his fourth wife.

Joanna must have fallen asleep on the bench in the park because when she awakened it was almost dark, the moon was very low in the horizon, all the other visitors had disappeared. In silence she walked up the main path towards The Long House, climbed up the myriad steps to the Bat Cave wondering why she was suddenly so spry, limber, having no hint of being impaired by rheumatoid arthritis.

She entered the cave, walking slowly towards the sound of restless flapping of wings. She stood quietly in a corner, able to see forms even in the blackness. She smelled an acrid humidity that made her press her nostrils together while her ears strained to hear the faint ticking, a language of sorts, a code, running from one shape to another, whipping them toward action, preparing them for the main event of the night, the search for nourishment. Her eyesight became more focused.

With an enormous sweep of synchronized wings, the bats flew out of the cave. Joanna pressed her back against the stone wall, covering her eyes with her hands, protecting them against the swell of wind. Soon there was only silence again and there was nothing to divine in the darkness, no forms outlined in all shades of black. She felt dismally alone. She retreated to the outside. Pressing her back against a rock wall, she slid to the ground, ending up in an upright, though curled up position, her arms wrapped around her knees, her head resting on her arms.

There was a scuttling sound nearby. Raising her head, she saw a small dark creature, a little like a shrew, looking at her with inky eyes with no luminosity. He was bent, his hind limbs splayed to one side, his nose was divided in two and pulled upwards into the shape of leaves. He was propped up on his hind limbs as if by crutches but as she observed more closely, she saw it was his own enormous hands, his folded wings, that kept him upright. Despite his awkwardness, his wings gave him an air of elegance. As he opened his mouth slightly, as if to speak, revealing triangular incisor teeth, she realized he was her very own leaf-nosed vampire bat, Zotz, the deity from the underground, the being who had come all the way from Yucatan, Mexico to meet her. She knew that she had dreamt him up. She knew that he was a guide in her quest. Who knows how long she and Zotz lost themselves in each other's image, never uttering a word, a sound. Perhaps they communicated in a soundless Morse Code.

A loud commotion interrupted their communication. Once again the swish of synchronized wings filled the air. The brown bats were swooping into their cave, returning to their roost after the hunt. Zotz motioned to her to follow him inside the cave. As she stood next to Zotz she realized they were the only oddities, the only strangers, the only aliens. Neither one of them belonged there with the brown bats.

Joanna had always felt like a foreigner everywhere she had lived. In Costa Rica she'd had to repeat kindergarten because of running away and returning home by herself. In the first and second grade, also in Costa Rica, she'd been made to stand on a tall stool in the middle of the whole class for poking her pencil into the palms of her hands. In Utah, when she was supposed to stand up to salute the flag, she stayed seated. In California she'd hung out with a runny-nose, bedraggled boy who everyone mocked. In Ohio, in the sixth grade she had torn up a Personality Book when it was her turn to write comments about her classmates, because she'd seen "Dirty Jew" written on Sonia Cohen's page. In Florida, in the eighth grade she got into a fistfight with some popular girls who were gossiping about a classmate. In Texas, in the ninth grade she had pretended to be all Mexican when she was in the Mexican class and pretended to be non-Mexican in the Anglo class. In New York City, when she had married at seventeen, she'd lied, saying she was still single or else she'd have had to finish high school at night. As a model, also in her teens, she'd acted as if she were a woman of the world, when in reality she came perilously close to being seduced into becoming a woman of the night. In her marriage to James, her identity had flitted back and forth among many roles: lover, muse, savior, mother, whore, child, cripple.

Still standing in the bat cave, she suddenly smelled something like ammonia in the air, large amounts of ammonia that choked her and bleached livid white spots on her arms and hands. She felt as if she were drowning in a lake of bad air. It was as if she'd fallen to the bottom of the cenote. Coughing violently, losing sight of Zotz, Joanna rushed out of the cave, continuing to cough till she thought her throat was being ripped apart. Too many bats, too much family, too many secretions and excretions. The atmosphere in the cave had been polluted, poisoned by the bats themselves.

When she recovered sufficiently she immediately searched for Zotz, but he was nowhere to be seen. He had disappeared. She began to descend the many steps to the plateau below, now baby-stepping all the way, no longer spry and limber. She walked slowly and painfully on the winding path leading to the parking lot, stumbling over uneven ground, past the bench where she had sat in the afternoon. Finally reaching her car she saw she had a ticket for not having left at sunset. Though it was still the night, she knew it would soon be a new day. Getting into the car, she turned on the headlights. What was that in front of her? Leaving the headlights on as she got out of the car, she rushed breathlessly up to the fence, tottering a little, almost losing her balance. There in front of her was the little vampire bat, totally white, having been bleached by the urinous ammonia in the cave, hanging upside down by his hand claws, both stiff wings stretched out to the side, his mouth open, once again, as if to speak, as if about to say the words that were never formed, as if to express the feelings that could not be voiced. "Look long and well at me! I am demonstrating with my own life with my own death, that you must ask and answer your own questions, that you must find your own way home, whatever it is, wherever it is to be found, or you will be as doomed as I have been. I, a leaf-nose vampire bat from the jungles of the Yucatan, Mexico, can never be a brown bat from New Mexico. I could only be who I was, or die."

HUNGER

One evening Joanna was left with Olinda, the housekeeper, while her father and mother went out. She was about four years old and she insisted on staying in the kitchen with Olinda while she cleaned up after dinner. She loved sitting on the blue tiled floor playing with pots and pans. Olinda asked her several times to stop banging them around, but she pretended not to hear. She asked Joanna to go to her playroom but she shook her head, refusing to leave her side. She chanted, "Tambores grandes, tambores chiquitos! Big drums, little drums!" She became so absorbed she didn't notice that Olinda had left the room. She was alone, but before she could become scared she heard giggling and murmuring in the pantry. She crept up to the closed door, got down on the floor and tried to look through the crack, but the opening wasn't as wide as the one in her mother's bedroom. Banging rhythmically on the pantry door she sang, "Tambores grandes, tambores chiquitos!"

Olinda finally emerged, smiling, quickly closing the door behind her, "I have a surprise for you, Joancita; go to the playroom; I'll be right there and you'll see what it is!" At first Joanna didn't budge; she didn't believe Olinda's smile; she thought she'd caught a glimpse of someone else behind her in the pantry. Could it be the devil Olinda often talked about, the one coming to punish her for all her badness?

Suddenly frightened Joanna ran to the playroom. She should never have instructed her baby sister to paint on the wall next to her crib with her own earthy substances; how terrible of her to climb out of her bedroom window, sliding down to the garden on the smooth flowering vines; it was not good to disturb mama when she was sleeping, perching herself on top of her until she awakened. Mama did enjoy cuddling with her but only when she wanted, only when she'd call her, holding her while she sang 'La Vida es un Sueño, Life is a Dream' or some other song of lamentation, tears wetting her face.

"Porque lloras, mama? "Why do you weep?

"I cry for all the mamas who can't have their children close to their hearts."

"Why can't they?"

"Because the little ones have gone to heaven."

"Why?"

"Because they didn't have enough to eat."

Joanna couldn't understand; how was this possible? There was so much food everywhere in their house, bowls of fruit, candies, baskets of sweet rolls, crispy loaves of bread in the dining room and kitchen.

As she sat rocking violently on her rocking chair in the playroom, Olinda showed up, leading some kind of a demon by the hand. Joanna stopped rocking, pressing her hands down hard on the arms of the chair.

"Joancita, meet my friend Octavio; don't you love his costume?"

Joanna nodded, not looking up, waiting. Suddenly Octavio was right in front of her. He was short with an enormous headdress which encased his head and upraised arms though of course she didn't know this at the time. His pretend face was painted on his belly, the face of a man-leopard with a huge open mouth with long fangs.

In a tiny, trembling voice she asked, "Why is your mouth so big?"

"So I can carry off children who misbehave."

Beginning once again to rock, she continued, "What do you do to them?"

"I eat them."

"Do you eat dead children, too?"

"What!"

"Do you eat children in heaven who didn't have enough to eat?"

Suddenly Octavio tore his headdress off, releasing his arms; Joanna was totally surprised; his real face was pleasant, very brown with small delicate features. Olinda began to laugh heartily, as Octavio blurted out, "What is it with this kid? Es una loca! She's crazy!"

Still laughing, Olinda stepped forward, taking her hand, "Come on Joancita, off to bed you go and don't you dare tell your padres about Octavio!"

As soon as she was tucked in, she sprang up again, grabbing Olinda's arm, "Don't go, please don't go—un abraso, un abraso!" She pleaded, stretching her arms up to her.

"Shhh, don't be silly! Now go to sleep!" And Olinda left, smiling, but not because of Joanna.

THE FAMILY WASH

Recently, whenever Joanna looked into the mirror in her bathroom, without turning on the light, and she peered at her shadowy self, she saw someone else. She was reminded of someone from her childhood in Costa Rica, someone who was brown, wrinkled, with round inquisitive eyes. She remembered who she was—it was the washerwoman, Okra. She called her Señorita Chon because she couldn't pronounce Joanna. Joanna liked looking out on their back patio, from a corner of the kitchen watching her rubbing their clothes on a scrub board in a large sink. But what she particularly liked was how, afterwards, she'd gingerly put the clothes through the wringer of the washing machine, the one she shunned, preferring the scrub board. Joanna loved watching the clothes coming out flattened, not dripping in the least, then being shaken back into life by Okra's strong arms and hands. Joanna was mesmerized by her humming, as she worked, its resonance sending vibrations through the air, all around her.

One day Okra spoke to her, as if she had eyes on the back of her head, "Señorita Chon, you don't have to hide from me; come here and sit on my stool." It was the one she rested on, from time to time, sitting very still, very straight, her eyes closed, a smile on her face. Joanna sat on the high stool, feeling on display, exposed—it was like the one used in her first grade class as punishment, where the culprit had to stand, in the middle of the whole class. She pulled at her skirt, attempting to hide her knees.

"Señorita Chon, what have you done to your knees?" she exclaimed, noticing the child's bloody abrasions and blackish bruises. Wiping her hands on her apron and adjusting the print scarf, wound tightly around her head like a turban, she added, "Wait here, I'll fix them right up!" and she ran into the house, returning with a little bottle and some bandages. Joanna was embarrassed, as if she'd done something on purpose to get attention. Okra washed her knees with water, then applying the stinging orange liquid, followed by the bandage, she asked, "How on earth did you do this?"

Sheepishly she told her how she had run down the steep slope near their house at full speed and had fallen, how she had disobeyed orders to never open the gate and go outside by herself.

"Ohhh, but no matter what, once you got hurt, you should have gone to your mother, la Señora Benita!" Joanna shrugged her shoulders, not answering, making a "mueca," a very extreme grimace. Okra continued, "A child must always go to their mama when they're in pain." Joanna still said nothing. Okra then returned to her work saying, "Why don't you go and play; you don't have to keep me company if you don't want to!"

Joanna jumped off the stool. How did Okra know she wanted to go? She looked closely at her face and saw, by its peacefulness, that it was really okay to leave, that she wasn't going to be aggrieved, accusatory, full of doleful regrets. The very next time Okra came to work, she skipped into the back patio and jumped up on the stool laughing, "My knees are all better!"

"That's good señorita! You're looking mischievous—what have you been up to?"

"Nothing, I was just up in mama's sewing room."

"Oh, and what did you do up there?" she asked, frowning, turning to carefully look the girl over.

"Nothing!" Joanna exclaimed playfully.

"What are those marks on your arms?"

"Nothing, nothing!"

Okra grunted a little, and saying nothing further, she returned to her work. Joanna was disappointed; she had said little about the reddish pinpricks she had given herself up and down both of her arms. For several weeks she didn't go near Okra. Then one day, when she was in her playroom, rearranging all her books and toys, once again, Okra came in and sat on a chair and just looked at Joanna. Though she was uncomfortable, she was happy Okra was there. Joanna smiled.

"Let me tell you a story, Señorita Chon. I once knew a family, far away from here, where the father was a fierce hunter. He hunted not for food but for fun. One day he brought home a baby python he had killed; he skinned it, dried out the skin and gave it to his little son as a toy, a plaything. The boy hung it on the back of a chair but now and then he'd drape the skin around himself and slither along the floor, whimpering and moaning. Shortly afterwards a huge python came into the boy's playroom through an open window. It was the baby python's mother. She swallowed the boy, not killing him, not eating him, not hurting him in the least, just carrying him off, safe and sound, within her body, and then she had disappeared back out through the window."

Joanna was excited, fascinated, but she could only exclaim "Oh!" However, she did feel a sense of balance about the story, almost as if it were one of those mathematical equations her father was always trying to drum into her head: father and son are the same as big python and little python; so big python minus little python equals father minus son. She could not understand anything further about the story, that there could be another equation: father hurts son; son suffers; mother comes to his rescue.

Rising from her chair, preparing to leave, Okra said, "Never, never hurt yourself because you are sad. Speak up, cry, scream your lungs out! Someone will be there for you."

OUT ON A LIMB

Joanna would have loved to have known the word "pendiculate" when she was in kindergarten because she had always been a smart-ass. Back then she would have wanted to shout, totally out of turn, in the middle of a lesson, "I'm now going to pendiculate from the tree."

As it was, in reality, she hadn't said anything; she had just scrambled up the smooth barked cherry tree growing in the middle of the school patio and swayed, pendiculated, to and fro, on a limb, looking down at all her classmates and her teacher, sitting nicely on their little chairs. She could stay up the tree for hours, not even responding to Miss Pendergast's lure, cream-filled bon-bons, which she had never offered to anyone else.

It all started during the Costa Rican version of *Show and Tell* which basically was just *Tell*.

"I'll bet you'll never guess what I did!" Joanna had exclaimed happily.

"Nooo!" The children responded in unison.

"Something only big people do," she continued.

"Tell us, tell us!"

"Well," Joanna said, puffing her chest up and out, "*I* had a baby."

Miss Pendergast opened her mouth, surprised, but then she quickly said, "you mean you got a new doll?"

"No, a real baby!"

"Now, don't be silly, Joanna, you're only five years old; you can't be a mama—only in pretend!"

"I did *so* have a baby—a real one! Come home with me and

I'll show you!"

"Ohh—you're pretending your newborn sister is yours, right? What a tease you are!"

"She's mine, only mine; she came out from here!" and she spread her legs apart and put my hands on her lower abdomen.

"That's enough! Shame on you! Go and sit down immediately! No playtime for you!"

That's when Joanna started to climb the cherry tree; that's when she became a pendulum marking the passage of time; when she made herself heaven while the others were only earth; when she became the biblical she-demon Lilith while her replacement Eve, lay by her mother's soft fluffy body back home; that's when she became the succubae pouncing on anybody who climbed up the tree to force her down, her long copper-colored hair covering her face, giving her the faceless look of someone from the underworld.

One day when Joanna was once again up the tree, Miss Pendergast softly pushed a little girl to a spot on the patio just below her, "Tell her, tell her!" she urged.

"I gave birth too!" Marlena sang out.

"See, see!" Joanna shouted, "It's possible!"

"Go ahead," Miss Pendergast said, "Tell her!"

"Well, papa and mama gave me something special to drink."

"Yes? What was it?" Joanna queried, frowning, "Why did they give it to you?"

"I had pains and they were worried." Then, beginning to giggle slightly, her long curls bouncing, Marlena continued, "It wasn't a baby, it was *worms*, a big pile of squiggly white worms—yuk!" and Marlena ran off, leaving Miss Pendergast sneering up at Joanna, her arms folded across her chest, "Come down here immediately, you little liar! Your mother's coming to take you home and you can expect to be punished!"

Brushing her hair off her face, Joanna lay down on the limb, her face against the hard smoothness, her tears making the bark gleam. "My baby has died," She murmured to herself.

Is this why she never had a child? Is this why she is fascinated by the Mexican Goddess of Childbirth, Tla-Col-Teutl, who has appeared at every critical crossroad of her entire long life carrying the cadaver of a baby?

FREE AS THE WIND

JOanna envied the two brothers who lived a few blocks away, near her school. They both lived on hills but they were hills apart. They went to public school, she to a private one. She'd seen them, as she walked with her nursemaid, on her way to school and back, in front of their house, their bicycles, scooters and skates scattered across their front yard. They had no fence, no gate; their front door was always wide open.

Telling her nursemaid to wait for her a block ahead, she sometimes lurked behind after school, watching them. The oldest boy was a few years older; perhaps he was eight or nine—she was six. Everyone called him Lolito and he had flaming red hair. His younger brother was her age and not as loud. He was called Manuel and his hair was a dull brown. They knew that she watched them; they didn't seem to mind. One day she overheard them talking, as they cleaned their bicycles, "You know Lolito, I bet I can beat out the fast express train!"

"Oh yeah, no way, but I can! You know I can pedal faster than you—I'm stronger! I'm older than you!"

At first she couldn't figure out what they were talking about but soon after, with her nursemaid in tow (threatening to tell on her), she began to look for train tracks, nearby. Finally she found them, at the foot of the steepest of all streets. Could they really race downhill and beat out the train as it crossed the street?

How lovely to be free enough to be able to even consider such a feat. She would be afraid, not of the train but of the possible disapproval of her father and mother, especially her father. One day she asked him, "Why can't I go in and out of the house through an open gate?"

"It's not safe."

"What can happen?"

"We're foreigners here in Costa Rica; I'm American, your mother Mexican; there are those who don't want us here."

"What would they do to me?"

"Well, they could grab you, take you away and then ask for money to get you back—you know I'm the big jéfe at the airport!"

She pondered and pondered. Her father hadn't said anything about the possibility of *her* doing anything bad, if she could go through the gate whenever she wanted, without her nursemaid. She was confused about freedom in general. He didn't allow her to go to church with some of her friends; he said he wanted her to remain free of people who wanted to capture her mind and never let it go, that she had to remain free to make up her own mind when she was big. It seemed that the only thing he was worried about was her being captured in some way or other. Was she then free to do anything else? He wouldn't have minded, if she had had a bicycle, that she ride it down a steep hill, as fast as the wind, faster than the fastest express train?

She began to watch the brothers every day, until she heard them finalize their plan, their competition. They were going to cut school that very day because the fast express train was scheduled to come through the nearby crossing around noon. Joanna sneaked out of her school and became an audience of one for Lolito and Manuel. They smiled at her, as if they knew her, as if they wanted her to admire them. Looking in her direction, Manuel said loudly, "Is everyone ready to see who's the fastest?"

Giving Manuel a contemptuous look, and in an even louder voice, probably for her benefit, Lolito said, "There's no way you can be faster than I!"

"Ha! You'd be surprised!" the younger brother answered.

"Well, if I left with as much spare time as you do, of course

I'd make it!"

Ignoring his brother's remark and quickly getting on his bike Manuel exclaimed, "I hear the train in the distance! Let's get ready!"

"Sure!" Lolito said, not making a move.

The roar of the train became louder and louder; Manuel yelled, "Off we go!" as he started down the hill.

"Ninny!" Lolito shouted after him, only then mounting his bicycle, slowly, taking his time, turning to smile at Joanna triumphantly. "See, no extra time for me!" And then he took off like a "flecha," an arrow.

The train's whistle pierced her ears. Was Lolito really going to make it? There he was already halfway across the tracks but there came the train. He *must* make it! She clenched her teeth, ground them, closing her eyes. Then the brakes screeched. She opened her eyes. People were gathering at the crossing. The train was stretched out across the street, panting and smoking. Joanna ran down the hill and tried to elbow her way to the tracks. Someone held her back, "There's nothing here for the eyes of a child!" She caught a glimpse of Manuel, kneeling by the tracks, in shock. Then another voice could be heard, "He almost got across but the train hit the rear fender, spun him around and rammed him in, right between the wheels!"

After recovering from her anguish, what did she think of Lolito's freedom? At the time, and for a long time after, she still admired it.

If They Could Speak

Long ago, when Joanna was about five years old, she sat all alone on the grass, in the enclosed garden and she was happy; no father teaching her about numbers or how to spell long words, no mother nagging her about her sassiness, no younger sister wanting her to play "house" with her, no baby sister bellowing out the loudest cry she'd ever heard. Even though she was surrounded by her clown, a giraffe and a miniature rocking horse, she wasn't doing anything whatsoever. She was just feeling the morning breeze coming all the way from the mountains outside San José, Costa Rica, all the way from where her best friend Wences lived. She was enwrapped in a timid sunlight knowing it had already reached Wences as he swam in the waterhole on his family's farm. She closed her eyes imagining herself there with Wences, his brother Herman and his three sisters, chewing on sugarcane stalks.

Suddenly she heard someone sighing. She opened her eyes and saw a boy who seemed to be around her age. He was sitting close by on the sidewalk, just on the other side of the wrought iron bars that made up the tall fence. His face was smudged as if he'd slept under an oxcart in the red mud of the hills, his trousers and shirt torn as if a goat or a wild dog had been yanking at them. She saw that he was carefully lining up ten, gray tin soldiers; strangely enough they were all headless. Scrambling closer to the bars she asked, "Where did their heads go?"

"I don't know—", the boy answered, shrugging his shoulders.

Sitting up on her knees and putting her head up against, and between the bars, so she could see better she continued, "Why do you keep them like that?"

"I don't know. I found them," he responded, knocking the soldiers down with one blow.

"Why don't you make heads for them?"

"What for?"

"So they can see, hear, smell and talk."

The boy carefully lined them up again, upright, this time in a circle instead of a straight line, "Don't be silly," he chuckled softly, "They'll never be able to do all that!" They're just tin!"

"I could make heads for them!" Joanna exclaimed, stretching for one of the soldiers through the bars, as the boy drew them all together, away from her reach.

"Oh yeah, out of what?"

"Oh, I don't know—Oh, I know, with gum and pebbles and I could use some of my own hair."

The boy laughed raucously, "That's silly!"

"Then, can I have them, please!" She urged tightening her hold on the bars, holding her breath.

The boy frowned, thinking, for what seemed a very long time, and then he murmured, "What will you give me?"

"My clown?" She liked it the least because he was always grinning at her.

"Not enough! How about the rocking horse too?"

Joanna hesitated. She had always loved to send it wildly rocking, ready to gallop off to far places. But as she glanced over once again at the puddle of helpless forms, she said, "Okay!"

"Not enough! I want the giraffe too!"

Could she part with her spotted friend, the one who glanced at her shyly, lovingly under long lashes? "Yes, yes," she finally said to herself, "the soldiers need me more!" And then, soon after, their transaction, their exchange came to a happy end, for both of them.

Perhaps if Joanna had had a calling in that direction, she could have been a sculptor, instead of a collector of statues from around the world, all symbols of people she'd known, or of places she'd been to. They all had a voice but the one that spoke to her the loudest every morning, as the first light of day reached it, was a little music box that her friend Eliseo had given her a year before he died. When he had given it to her, it only played a little tune upon being lifted–it didn't have a key to wind up—it was only a little ceramic Russian Cupola that had come with a bottle of vodka. It didn't really fit with all the statues on the shelves, and so, after Eliseo died, she had placed it, on its side, on a bottom shelf, near a window. That's when it began to sing to her, as the new day touched it, the warmth of the light bringing it to life—that's when she began to answer as the song came to an end, "Good morning, dear man!"

EROS IN THE DOLL HOUSE

She was Joancita back then, little Joan or Joanna. She looked out of her window watching the rain. The drops came down heavily like clear stones. If only it would rain all day, tonight and tomorrow so she wouldn't have to go to school to her first grade class. Half asleep, she watched as some drops slipped quietly into the red roses while others skated on the leaves. Before long the necklaces of clear stones turned into strings that twisted around each other. The roses began to look like cracked cups full of boiling water. She was remembering how only yesterday she had run round and round the block trying to get home while Pépe chased her with his fists ready. Just as she thought she was safe, her front gate only a few feet away, he had appeared before her, crouching, black eyes gleaming. She had run to one side, then to the other but she couldn't get through. Then despite her wanting to seem not to care, to just look as if it was all great fun, she had cried. She never had before, even when Pépe had trapped her in the play corner of their classroom where a little house had been built containing child-sized living-room furniture and family dolls, father, mother and children dolls. He hadn't spoken. He'd grabbed her from behind, one arm around her neck, and with the other he'd punched her wherever he could reach. He did this quietly, and then pretended nothing happened, offering her a pretend cup of coffee or a pretend piece of fudge.

Remembering how she had cried, she covered her face and put her head down on the windowsill. She couldn't tell her mother and father because they'd insist once again she be escorted to and from school. It had taken so much effort to convince them she could handle herself like a big girl. She cringed, shivering all over remembering how upon seeing her cry Pépe had rushed up to her, real close, in the street near her gate and, grabbing her in a rough embrace he'd caressed the side of her chest with his knuckles and then he'd run off.

The rain suddenly stopped. She knew she had to go to school. There was only one thing to do and that was to be prepared for Pépe; she would not cry in front of him again. All that morning in class he glanced in her direction, smiling, though sometimes frowning, rubbing his fingers against the hard edges of his desk. After eating lunch she went to the foot of the ball field, by the crudely made wall of stone and filled her lunch pail with rocks. It was heavy. Good. She practiced swinging her arm back and forth to loosen and strengthen her muscles. The pain felt good. She was ready for Pépe.

As soon as the class was dismissed, she started to walk as quickly as possible, pretending she wanted to avoid him, looking around, her eyes opened wide, her mouth gaping in pretend fright. He was nowhere. Then as she rounded the last corner there he was, blocking her path. He stared at her with his big eyes, biting the insides of his cheeks. He stood like a wrestler, legs apart, arms loose and ready. He was large for a boy of six, tall and stocky. She'd heard he helped his father after school working in the meat market, going everywhere with him, even to cantinas late at night. Suddenly Pépe looked down and began to stroke the sidewalk with the heel of one of his shoes. She started to walk past him. Perhaps she'd get even some other day. But then he jumped in front of her, a peculiar twist to his mouth, almost as if he were trying to smile. She didn't know what to do but as he stepped towards her, his eyes blinking, she swung her pail at him, and as the metal was about to strike him full in the face he let out a cry, a startled pained cry, knocking the pail from her hand. The top came off, the rocks rolling around their feet. He was breathing hard, his face crinkled, pale. She stepped back, alarmed, but Pépe only opened his mouth, closed it again and ran away.

Many weeks passed. Pépe ignored her the way he'd always ignored everyone else. Whenever the teacher spoke to him he looked past her as if she wasn't there or as if he were too far away to hear her. Joanna began to feel sorry as if she'd done something wrong. She wanted to say something nice to him but what could that be? When she felt bad at home she'd make out a mental list right before going to sleep of all her faults, mainly about angering her mother and disappointing her father; he thought she wasn't learning fast enough; he wanted her to be way ahead of everyone else in her class and so to this end he gave her private lessons almost every day, giving her more and more difficult books to read. To appease her mother she'd just pray to be nicer. To appease her father she'd tell him over and over how much she loved their grueling sessions.

She knew what she must do about Pépe. One day she slipped a note to him asking him to meet her in the doll corner after they'd completed their math class assignment. She spread her skirt neatly to the sides of her as she sat on the little armchair, her knees and feet together in a symmetrical way. She had put on her best socks, the ones with the lace ruffles at the top, and she'd tied her braids up on top of her head with one of her mother's ornamental hair clips. Pépe entered the little house, looking at her warily. Joanna smiled. He approached her. She kept on smiling. He came up close, almost touching her knees, looking down at her, a tiny smile on a corner of his lips, his arms by his side, waiting.

"I miss you," she began. "You haven't run after me in a long time."

Pépe smiled a little more, shrugging his shoulders.

"You can hug me if you like, you can even kiss me," she continued, speaking as sweetly and earnestly as she could.

The Big Playmate

Joanna was ten and her father was soon to go overseas to help rebuild airports in war-torn France. Her parents had made friends with another Captain and his wife at the Air Force base in California. Captain Ned had black hair, full lips, long lashes and a mischievous smile when he looked at Joanna. She loved it when the family visited him and his wife because he had an attic where she and her two younger sisters would play Hide and Seek with him in total darkness. She had seen the attic once in the daylight and knew that the dusty low ceiling room was full of antique furniture, cushions, drapes and quilts. But what had intrigued her was a dress mannequin standing in a corner. Ned's wife had told her that it had been made with her measurements long ago when she was thinner. Joanna had noticed that she had an enormous cleavage when she wore low-cut dresses but Ned never seemed to notice, unlike her father who was always surreptitiously trying to touch her mother either on her buttocks or around her ample breasts. Whenever Joanna looked at her own naked body in a mirror she couldn't imagine how her chest could ever become so inflated.

One evening when they were all at play, up in the attic, Joanna hid behind the headless mannequin, while her sisters went squealing off in the opposite direction. After a long time she felt Ned's presence in the dark; she heard his stealthy footsteps, his steady soft breathing, a little like the sound of a light spring breeze, bringing with it an aroma of cloves and cinnamon. Then she felt more than saw his hands sliding over the mannequin, from the chest, down to the indented waist, then enveloping the hips. "Are you here? Is this you? No, it can't be; this is not a child! Where are you? Surely you haven't grown up that fast!" Joanna wondered how Ned knew it was her and not her sisters? Could he see in the dark? Could he smell her out the way their black police dog Rex used to do in their old neighborhood? But then dogs were different; they had special senses that human beings didn't have. Maybe Ned was not totally human. She was enchanted by the idea of handsome dark-haired men who became transformed into bats or wolves.

Joanna drew away from Ned's hands into a corner as he reached beyond the mannequin and lunged at her. She screamed and tried to run for the door but instead she ran right into his outstretched arms; he swooped her off her feet and into the air, the encircling strong arms taking her breath away. "I won, I won!" Ned shouted, "You can't hide from me!"

Her sisters came out of hiding, "No fair; you never even tried to find *us*!" And they jumped on Ned's back beating on him. Putting Joanna down he exclaimed, "Okay, okay! *You* won! Now let's go and see about dinner!"

Afterwards they all sat in the living room listening to the radio—something about General Eisenhower. Ned sat opposite Joanna in a large lounging chair, one leg bent, up on the seat. She had no idea what she was looking for, or what she saw, or what even motivated her to look in that direction, but suddenly she was staring at Ned's crotch. Then looking up at his face she saw he was smiling at her. Suddenly Joanna was overcome by an all-absorbing, deep shame that has never left her when she remembers the incident. Why?

Is this the moment when Joanna should remember the shower she took with her father when she was four? When she was forced by her mother to accompany him to New York from Costa Rica to visit his estranged mother and she'd become not only homesick but horribly seasick? Probably, desperately attempting to console her, as well as to clean her up, Keith had taken her into the shower with him. Frightened by the strangeness of a shower, having only known bathtubs, Joanna had crouched down, hiding her face, rubbing her eyes. Her father had picked her up, raising her up to the showerhead. She began to laugh. When he lowered her, she demanded "*otra vez, otra vez*! again, again!" She had become intoxicated with the magic of strong hands, the power of the blinding waterfall, the transportation into space.

Could this exhilarating experience at four be connected with her shame at ten? Had she felt something about Ned when he lifted her that reminded her of something she had also felt about her father? What do you think? But still, no matter what, why does she still feel such shame when she remembers Ned's crotch?

THE CHIMERIC SELF

Long ago in Brownsville, Texas there were two separate classes in the high school—one for Mexicans and one for Anglos. Since Joanna's Mexican mother had taken her to register, she was put into the Mexican class. She wondered if she would have been put into the Anglo class if her Irish-English father had been the one with her on that day.

She hated how she looked on the first day of school, long curls and a rustling dress. Though she was fourteen, her mother thought she was still a child. But it didn't take long before Joanna began to brush out her curls, on the way to school, till her hair hung in long waves around her shoulders. She applied lipstick, unbuttoned the top three buttons of her dress and removed her silk socks. By the end of her first week she'd made friends with Lupe; she reminded Joanna of an umbrella fir tree with her Afro of thick curly hair and her long lean body. Lupe was like a magical tree living serenely in a special place. The rest of her classmates came into class looking tired and rumpled, perhaps from long hours of wage-earning work after school.

Joanna watched Lupe closely, looking for a stray hair, a streak of dust or a frown, but finding none she continued to feel calm and comfortable in her presence. "I love your hair," Lupe would say to her, "You look like a movie star!" Other times she'd run her fingers through Joanna's hair saying, "It's so silky; I wish I had hair like yours!"

"No," Joanna would laugh. "Your hair is perfect!"

One Saturday she decided to visit Lupe unannounced. She sneaked out of the house without telling anyone where she was going. She missed Lupe. She walked down the avenue between tall palm trees and two-story white houses. Then she passed narrower streets with small houses. As she walked further the houses became dark, the trees becoming shaggy brush. She imagined Lupe's house would be a tiny cottage hidden among the weeping willows surrounded by flowers. It didn't matter if it was on a dusty unpaved road. She came to the number she sought at the end of the road, on a burnt-looking house, surrounded by chickens pecking at sparse grass. But no, it wasn't Lupe's house. She was told the house she was seeking was in the back at the end of a narrow alleyway. But as she walked all the way down the alley, all she saw was a tiny, square tin hut with not a tree or bush or flower in sight. She saw a girl washing her hair in a tub of water placed on a tree stump. The ground around her was cleanly swept, the marks of a broom still freshly imprinted, the aroma of wet earth in the air. She saw that the girl's feet were bare, muddy, scratched up. She must have been the one who had swept the ground. Her sundress was torn under the arms as if it had long ago been outgrown. The hem had been let out roughly, leaving little threads hanging here and there. The girl must be poor, Joanna thought. She must be someone's servant girl like the ones their family had in Latin America. Perhaps the girl would know where Lupe's house was. It could be she had the wrong address.

As she approached the girl Joanna saw that her bare back was full of tiny red pimples, all with little crowns of pus. She backed away. Perhaps she had a contagious disease. At that moment the girl straightened up, raised her head, wrapping her hair in a faded towel. It was Lupe. Joanna gasped. They looked at each other frowning. Lupe pushed her shoulders further back, raising her head high on her long neck as she calmly asked, "How are you? What are you doing in these parts?"

"I'm sorry. I shouldn't have come!"

Lupe threw the cloth down onto the ground, shaking her head vigorously, the water splattering all over them. Laughing, Lupe looked straight into Joanna's wet face and taking her elbow she firmly guided her to the hut, "I want you to meet my mother."

Lupe's mother was enveloped in smoke in a corner of the one-room hut. The rich aroma of saffron rice and black beans with garlic was everywhere. It was her favorite food, though her mother hardly ever prepared it anymore, thinking it was too lowly for her family.

"So, this is your Joancita, tu princesa! Stay dinner, no? Por favor, será nuestro gusto!"

Joanna winced; she could hardly speak English just like her own mother. The frayed black straps of her brassiere were visible under the pink transparent blouse, revealing overflowing breasts. Her black hair was carefully braided into two plaits that hung on her back all the way down to her waist. Her face was soft; she smiled through glowing eyes.

"Lo siento, pero me esperan en casa!" (I'm sorry but I'm expected at home.) Joanna was surprised to hear herself speaking Spanish. Ever since she'd come to the U.S. and had quickly learned English at nine, Joanna hadn't spoken a word of Spanish. She was puzzled. She liked Lupe's mother; she was poor, uneducated, but, unlike mama, she was confident, content.

Lupe scowled as she sat down on the bed, idly playing with the tassels of the cover, her eyes cast downwards. Joanna stood awkwardly, looking around. She saw Lupe's three dresses, puffed out with starch, hanging in a corner, looking totally out of place among the old, crude fly-specked furniture. Inadvertently, she shook her head.

"Let's go!" Lupe exclaimed, jumping to her feet, "I'll walk you to the main road."

Once outside Joanna put her arm around Lupe's shoulder, holding her tenderly, leaning a little on her body. "I like your mother! She really loves you! She takes such good care of you!"

Lupe didn't respond but didn't move away from Joanna's touch. They walked on, aware of the soothing warmth of each other's body. Upon reaching the boulevard Lupe turned to look at Joanna's face, her eyes sparkling. Joanna wanted to embrace her, to tell her she was glad that she had come, that everything would be okay, that she looked forward to seeing her on Monday. But instead she heard herself say in a voice she hardly recognized, a vacuous, saccharine voice, "Poor, poor Lupe, you deserve a better life!"

Lupe pulled away violently, and then she began to run back to her house, the displaced dust forming little clouds, tiny pebbles shooting out behind her. Joanna stood looking at her, rooted to the spot, saliva gushing into her mouth, her heart pounding in her temples, her stomach turning upside down. She had no idea how she got home. She went straight to bed. On Monday she was unable to go to school; she had the flu with a high fever.

Feeling both like the betrayer and the betrayed, she remained ill in her bed for three weeks. Finally, when she was well, her father put Joanna into the Anglo class, thinking that this was what his daughter wanted.

SNAKE WITH THREE NOSES

"Papa, tell me again about the viper!" Joanna exclaimed, putting down her homework on the coffee table. Lowering his newspaper, *The New York Daily Compass*, he chuckled softly. She loved these early evenings when she was fifteen when her mother and her two younger sisters were busy in the kitchen preparing dinner. She loved sitting on the living room couch with him even when they didn't talk. She could feel he was as aware of her as she was of him. She liked that he seemed taller when he was sitting down, his long strong torso compensating for his short legs. His smile still revealed one gold tooth whenever he admired her long legs, her flowing brown hair with streaks of russet which must have reminded him of the Irish side of the family, his father's siblings, the glamorous professional gamblers. Sometimes Joanna had the impression her father loved quirkiness, maybe even badness, but other times he seemed so righteous, moral. He had even told her how he'd run away from home at fourteen because his mother couldn't believe he had been molested by a priest. It was the first time she had heard that a male did things to other males, but it was all still very confusing and she tried not to think about it.

"But I've told you about the viper over and over!"

"I don't care, tell me again!" Joanna drawled, sidling down the silken medieval tapestry pattern of the couch to put her head on his shoulder; he smelled of black tea and French cigarettes and it was always at this point that she felt like sucking her thumb, though of course she never did! Her father recounted how in the late 1920's when Pan American Airways had sent him to work a radio on top of a mountain in Mexico in order to guide airplanes through the turbulent air masses, he'd befriended a striped viper. He named it Tres Narices because he had three noses, a regular one and a double-chambered pit on each cheek for tracking down warm-blooded prey. This always made her smile; she knew her father was a lonely man even when he was with people, with family, and perhaps even when he was with her. Maybe that's why she'd sometimes sing to him "Canta y No Llores" (Sing, Don't Cry), hugging him, kissing him on both sides of his face during the "Ay Ay Ay" refrain; ever since he'd lost all his hair when he was five he'd felt freakish, inferior. (His mother was to blame because she had kidnapped him away from his beloved aunt who had mothered him since infancy). She'd caress his perfectly-shaped skull, patting down the soft wispy tufts of hair.

Springing up suddenly she puffed up the brightly colored pillows embroidered by her mother; then throwing them down closer to Keith, she bounced back down on the couch, returning her head to his shoulder, "Now tell me about you and Mama, you know, kissing and all that during the hurricane in Cozumel!"

Keith moved forward reaching for a cigarette, her head sliding abruptly off his shoulder, "I never should have told you that story in the first place; your mother keeps scolding me for talking to you as if we were equals, you know, not father and daughter; she insists it gives you a big head and license to lord it over her." Then after lighting his cigarette and taking a long puff, he continued, "Recently she told me something very strange, something I myself don't remember—that you've been contemptuous of her since you were four when you and I returned from a boat trip to New York from Costa Rica and you handed her your enormous bag of toys saying they belonged to her, not to you, as if you were the big one and she was the little one!"

"That's silly!" Joanna exclaimed, lightly hitting Keith's back, knowing his eyes were squinting in the clouds of smoke, little wrinkles circling his features. "She's just jealous!" But she was hurt by her mother's indirect accusations; she felt like crying, like

132

running into the kitchen and embracing her soft body but she didn't, she couldn't.

"Don't talk like that about your mother," her father retorted, standing up and facing her.

"Well, it's true! She's jealous I know so much; she's always putting me down—the other day she said I looked like a boy when she came into the bathroom while I was in the bathtub!" She knew she was long, lanky with small breasts while her sister Ana, who was thirteen, was already rounded, full-breasted, like their mother.

And then, much to her chagrin, Keith told her once again how Benita had only reached the fourth grade because during the ten-year long Mexican Revolution of 1910 the family had been on the run, trying to escape not only from government forces and opposing rebels, but also from their own people, Maya Indians on the rampage.

"You must try harder to be a kind daughter to her; you can't imagine what she had to endure when she was your age."

Perking up Joanna asked, "What happened to her? An illness, an accident, was she attacked in some way?"

"Nooo, not exactly. I'm sorry, I can't tell you—I promised Benita."

Keith ground out his cigarette with such fierceness that she jumped with alarm. Why was he so upset? Whatever happened to Mama was long before they ever met. Then she remembered another time when Keith had displayed the same kind of seething rage—when she'd gone to a high school dance, when she'd danced wildly with a young man from the street who'd crashed the party and Keith had appeared from nowhere, grabbing her arm and silently taking her home with him.

Somehow sitting there in the living room, looking up at her father she could feel just what he was feeling; it was a very familiar feeling, but like him, she didn't want to accept it, to acknowledge pure jealousy.

Slaughter in the Playroom

It was to be a secret ceremony. Joanna was to tell no one. She promised; it was the word "secret" that did it, bringing to mind play-acting, costumes, masks, riddles, shadows, hidden staircases.

As she headed for Lena's apartment on Central Park West where the ceremony to celebrate the fifth anniversary of her African-American Art Gallery was to be held, she wondered who else would be there. Would they be black or white or a mixture of the two? Since Lena disliked the doorbell, she tried her knocker first but the ancient lion's head only made a dull thud. She turned the knob—the door was unlocked. Cautiously she walked in; the shades were all drawn though it was the middle of the afternoon. She knew the three rooms well, the living room, dining room and bedroom, all full of large wooden and bronze statues, carved wooden furniture covered by animal skins, some still with heads and paws. Strewn about on the sideboards were skulls of monkeys, opossums and ocelots, conch shells and one glittering crystal ball, all strangely juxtaposed to paintings on the walls depicting modern life in New York, many of them with a Chagall-like whimsy or a Giacometti sense of inner and outer starvation. Hearing voices in the fourth room (unknown to her since it had always been closed during all of Lena's exhibition events), she approached the door. Lena had told her that it was meant to be a child's room, but that she used it for storage. "Come in!" the sign on the door commanded.

At first only two silhouettes could be seen, the profiles of a woman and a man, a kneeling slender figure with breasts and a tall standing one with a shapeless protuberance around the loins. Then, as Joanna's eyes became accustomed to the dark room, lit only by candles placed on benches against the back wall, she noticed that Lena wore only a bikini, that her Afro had been transformed into interlocking corn braids crowning her head. The man was a very dark black man with skin glistening with oil, wearing a diaper-like loin cloth; he held rattles in his hands as he prayed quietly.

"Meet my priest Azaro!" Lena sang out. "Azaro, meet my friend who is to be our witness."

Joanna knew she would be the only guest. Without even turning to acknowledge her, Azaro answered in a deep sonorous voice, "At last we can begin!"

As Joanna made her way to an empty space on a bench between flaming candles she felt uneasy, as if she didn't belong, as if she were an intruder. Azaro began to wave the rattles over Lena's head, chanting loudly. Then from behind what must have been a closet door Joanna heard subdued cackling voices. Were they mocking her? Suddenly she felt so white, *too* white; the brownness from her Maya Indian heritage was not visible. Even her Maya-Mexican mother hadn't affirmed it when she was born. She'd said that with her cream-colored skin, her dimples and her round yellow-green eyes, Joanna belonged to her father, that though she'd given birth to her, it was as if Joanna wasn't hers.

Azaro chanted even louder as he danced around Lena using the rattles as his musical accompaniment, his full loincloth seeming to do a dance of its own, while the shiny oils on his body became intermixed with his musky perspiration. Joanna could barely breathe. Then, throwing the rattles at her feet, still dancing and chanting, Azaro abruptly opened the thick closet door. The voices, the cackling became piercingly high-pitched as he pulled out a wooden crate. He opened it. Six small chickens were inside, yellow eyes popping out of their tiny heads, feathered arms flapping. Azaro grabbed one of them by its slender neck and with a swift movement he twisted the head right off, its last screech stifled.

Then turning the little twitching body upside down, Azaro poured the blood onto Lena's head as if the creature were a pitcher.

Joanna's heart grabbed at her throat. She thought she would faint but she didn't. She sat there transfixed as Azaro repeated the ritual five more times till Lena was painted red from head to toe. She smiled a smile of certitude that a wish would be fulfilled; was it that her gallery would be a greater success, or was it that a new life inhabit the room in the form of a baby that would be hers?

Slowly recovering from her benumbed state, Joanna wondered how much blood had been shed in mama's life, before she was born, to make her renounce her daughter, ever so subtly, for her whiteness.

THE WILDS OF SANTA ELENA

Back in the time of the Civil War in Quintana Roo, Mexico, in the 1920's, families who had Socialists as relatives fled to Santa Elena. Crocodiles came seeking dogs at doorsteps, tigers came to pastures killing cows and boas swallowed chickens and their eggs. This was Joanna's mother's childhood—arduous treks to Santa Elena, cowering in the jungle, losing one pet dog after another, her education disrupted, virtually eliminated, and then returning home to an increasingly more impoverished Chetumal.

In the early 1950's when Joanna, age twenty, and her two sisters, eighteen and fifteen, went to Mexico with their mother, the surround of Santa Elena still had crocodiles, tigers and boas but it had added one stone house to a town of mainly bamboo and mud huts. Nearby there were trees from which matchsticks were made, plants which could blind and snakes that were purported to chase women only. In a recently cleared patch in the jungle stood two statues that had just been excavated. One was of a woman garmented only by the coils of a snake, her head, her face was that of a fierce serpent. The other statue was of a twisted dwarf feathered from head to toe by the plumes of an eagle. Many said that La Bruja, The Witch, and El Enano, The Dwarf, represented two aspects of Mexico, the alluring, the captivating and the vulnerable. When asked what they thought was the meaning behind his garb of plumes they answered, "*Son las aspiraciónes.*" La Bruja and El Enano were Benita's deities as she was growing up.

Benita's father and brothers had no markers anywhere commemorating their deaths. The brothers Manolo and Reinaldo who were known as Nolo and Reni and their two much younger sisters Luisa and Benita were brought up primarily by their mother who was a full-blooded Maya, small, strong, the color of hazelnuts. Their Hispanic father, tall, light-skinned with thick black hair, was often away on endeavors so mysterious that to this day they could only guess what they could have been. Nevertheless Nolo, Reni and Benita, the "baby" of the family, adored their father and often sought him out in the cantinas he frequented when he did come home bringing money and gifts. They loved his gallant charming ways, so different from their severe dour mother. A self-educated, well-read man, he would rant and rave with eloquence about the chaos of Mexican politics since the Revolution of 1910, (the ineffectuality of the murdered Francisco Madero, the repressiveness of the overthrown Victoriano Huerta, the greatness but failures of Venustiano Carranza, Francisco Pancho Villa and especially of Emiliano Zapata, and he cried over the heroic attempts for agrarian and education programs partially implemented by Plutarco Elias Callas before he was assassinated). He seemed not to be aware of how cruelly neglectful he was being of his wife and four children. He took pride in consorting with outcasts, a Chinese man, a candy grocer who secretly operated an illegal gambling establishment, and a black man from a Caribbean island who smuggled guns into Mexico. The Chinese man was eventually murdered, cut up and stuffed into large tin cans. The black man was savagely assaulted and though left to bleed to death he survived, horribly maimed and mutilated by knives.

When Nolo was fifteen a handsome tall boy who looked like his father, *abuelita* sent him to British Honduras to buy supplies for her small store. Waylaid by fun-loving acquaintances he ended up hospitalized from fatigue and alcohol poisoning, the money gone, no supplies having been bought. Kicked out of his home he went to live in a hotel in Chetumal. There were only two, affectionately called The Sluthouse and The Slophouse. They were both near The Slaughterhouse where pigs were heard screeching like giant drills all night long. Eventually he moved in with an older woman, a long-legged, black beauty from British Honduras who cherished a special pet, a coral pink piglet with long golden hairs upon its back who cried all night like a human baby as he heard the death screams of his tortured brethren. At the age of seventeen Nolo and his woman disappeared never to be heard from again. It was believed they went to work in a *chicle* plantation in Central America where the pay was high but life was perilous, wild animals, insects and angry disillusioned people all around.

Reni, the youngest brother who was dark and short, taking after his mother fought in the Civil War in the 1920's (on the side of Carranza who was later deposed). While cleaning his rifle he accidentally killed two opposition soldiers being held as prisoners. He was tried, acquitted, exiled to the innermost land of the Maya, to Santa Cruz de Brava as the assistant to a hotheaded engineer who soon after shot the Indian Chief during an argument. As the engineer ran off he shouted to Reni to run also. Reni stood his ground answering "I've done nothing! Why should I run?" He was tied to a pole, fed garbage and excrement, stoned, burned by cigarettes. If the Chief died, so would he. The fact that Reni was half-Maya didn't help in the least, the Maya in that area abhorred the half-breed. The Chief survived and Reni was sent off by foot on an empty stomach and numb pained limbs. He too disappeared never to be heard from again.

Towards the end of our trip *abuelita* declared with great fervor that she was going to cook us a very special meal, "*Que contenta soy* that you're all here with me, but I'm *feliz, feliz* that you live far away from *este país tan terible!*" Then removing her Sunday shoes of a shiny leather she rushed out into her tiny yard and began to chase after the fattest of her scrawny chickens—her energy was so ferocious that the family and the visitors all burst out laughing. Her headscarf fell off, the buttons of her tight print dress went flying. Glowing with triumph, her wispy hair standing on end, her bare feet dusty she finally held the chicken by its neck. While everyone watched, Benita having already left the scene, *abuelita* twisted the creature's neck. Its orange eyes swelled, blood rushed from them and from its beak, its wings flapped wildly. *Abuelita* wrung its neck again but it continued flapping. Then she twisted one last time, her face contorted, flushed; the chicken quivered violently, claws stiffening, wings becoming petrified in mid-air. It had finally died but how it had fought to live! Even though it was cooked in a spicy chocolate sauce Benita and the three sisters weren't able to eat it. As they ate the rice only they apologized to *abuelita* telling her the heat was getting them down, unable to tell her outright that they were sick at heart, deeply repelled by the violence she had displayed with such relish, the cruelty towards a living thing. *Abuelita* ate heartily. Then putting down her utensils, wiping her mouth with her hand embroidered napkin she pronounced, "It would indeed be a sad state of affairs if we were all to mourn for chickens! Maybe where you live, that great America, is not as advanced as I had thought!"

As Joanna now remembered her mother at that time in her little pointed shoes with pompoms and her long hair held aloft by bejeweled hairclips, her delicate features expressing such disgust, such dread she knew she'd always been the same. How she must have disappointed *abuela* with her timid soul! No wonder *abuelita* had been relieved to see her get married to a gringo, their father. Supposedly he would be able to take Benita away from the land of the serpent-woman, the being who was forever frozen in a moment of transformation. He'd be able to shield her from the dwarf who, though bountifully plumed, could not get off the ground, could not fly.

THE COLD BREATH OF THE VOLCANO

The two grand but dormant volcanoes were part of a mountain range surrounding San José, Costa Rica. Poas was the closest. It called to the three sisters. It always had as they were growing up in San José but they hadn't known it. Perhaps they had been too young, too little. But now that they had returned to the land of their childhood they knew they must heed the call. They knew they must climb up to Poas' crater, to its opening, to its mouth. They must see what there was to be seen, what there was to be heard.

Joanna was twenty, Ana eighteen, Dolores fifteen and even though the three of them had not been together for the last three years they'd been in full accord about the climb.

One chilly misty summer morning while it was still dark, while their father and mother slept, they drove off with their guide Tomás to the foot of Poas. They hardly spoke. Only painted decorative wagons driven by oxen rumbled down the street towards the market carrying goods from far off *fincas*—sugar cane, coffee beans, bananas, milk. As soon as their car left the city limits all the roads led uphill. Once they were high enough the three of them turned their heads to look back at the lights of the town but a thickening mist dimmed their view. Strange but none of them had turned their head as they had passed the cemetery on the edge of town. They had a brother buried there who would have been sixteen, a year older than Dolores. He had only lived for a few days, perhaps four, and they often thought of him because his death had caused their mother an everlasting grief. Just recently they'd gone with her to visit the grave; a statue of an angel sat on one end, an inscription read, "May you be able to smell the sweet flowers and may you feel the cool breezes upon your beloved face." The three of them had glanced at each other. Was each one thinking that these words should have been bestowed upon the living? Were they wishing that such a benediction would have been directed towards them, long ago? But they didn't want to be blaming. There was much they didn't know or understand about their mother. For now it was the burnt out fires of Poas that intrigued them, fires they imagined could have illuminated the darkest, the foggiest of nights.

As they left the car at the side of the road the light of day was slowly emerging. It was also raining slightly. They put on their hooded rain jackets and placed their knapsacks on their backs. Tomás instructed them to stay behind him as he investigated the condition of the paths ahead. They could become treacherous with the rain. They didn't know too much about him, only that he worked on a mountain ranch for one of their father's old friends. He was lean, lanky, tanned, his skin craggy, his eyes soft, calm. They had immediately felt drawn to him; to his relaxed manner, so unlike their intense complicated father. They knew that at some point before their reunion came to an end they'd have to talk about the events that had torn the family apart three years before, leaving Joanna, a newlywed at seventeen, in New York and the rest of the family headed for England.

The light rain persisted.

Before long the path became soft, sticky. Then they were walking in mud up to the ankles of their knee-high hiking boots. As the daylight became stronger they saw fallen tree trunks, twisted branches, squashed leaves, berries, all around them in every direction as if a storm had just passed through. The climb was more difficult than they had anticipated, two steps up and one back again. Suddenly Tomás yelled at them to stay where they were. Before their eyes he began to sink into a mud hole. Soon he was immersed up to his waist. Joanna began to scramble around, slipping and sliding; she was trying to reach him; she wanted to pull him up and out of the hole. Ana and Dolores rushed to hold her back, Ana exclaiming, "What's the matter with you? What are you trying to do?" Though Joanna was taller, stronger, she allowed herself to be stopped. However, she looked with exasperation at Ana's clenched jaws and hands, the corners of her mouth turned downwards. Why did Ana always have to reflect the reality of things? Ana's artwork always depicted the calamities of the day, the Korean War, refugees, orphans, the death of the Rosenbergs. From afar they watched as Tomás slowly extricated himself and leaped forward onto firm ground by holding onto a thick branch hanging over his head. He laughed, "Well, we'll have to go up the long way after all; we'll have to corkscrew our way around and up. I had hoped we could go straight up!"

As they wound their way round and round, sometimes walking on almost level ground and sometimes going up steep slopes, Dolores stayed closer and closer to Joanna trying to imitate her long easy stride though *her* legs would never be as long as Joanna's. However, she was strong, well-balanced due to ballet lessons and she had a perseverance that Joanna envied, practicing her pirouettes over and over.

Once again Tomás motioned to them to wait. He came back to where they stood, "Part of the path ahead has been washed away. It's really narrow. We'll have to hold hands, make a chain and walk sideways staying up close to the face of the mountain." He went first, then Ana; Dolores and Joanna at the end. To make things worse it began to rain hard. The ground became a running stream of mud, the wall of the mountain a waterfall. But it felt good to be part of a linked chain; each could even turn their head and peer closely at the thick green and pink moss growing on the wall.

Still gripped together they stumbled onto a vast flat area, an oasis. Reluctantly disengaging themselves the three sisters stared with awe at the gigantic trees, at the encircling vines, the purple flowers with bulging orange centers. The prairie-like grass had dried dung here and there, probably from goats. They headed towards a run-down shed nearby, eager for a rest. Inside there was a crude wooden table, benches, a stone fireplace. While they ate their lunch of fried egg sandwiches and strawberry buttermilk that their hotel had packed for them, Tomás said he'd look over the path ahead. The pink buttermilk was what they'd always happily drank as they awakened when they had been children.

"Don't you sometimes wish we'd never left Costa Rica?" Joanna asked.

"I don't know; papa really needed to do his bit against Fascism," Ana began.

"Yeah, but it meant all of us moving to America, and then his leaving poor mama alone with no English, alone with the three of us while he went overseas," Joanna interrupted.

"It sounds as if you would have preferred to have stayed here! But then you wouldn't have met Tim, gotten married."

"I wish I'd never gotten married!" Joanna blurted out.

"So why did you?" Dolores asked. "I wish you'd have come with us; so why did you?"

"Because papa threw that chair at me, remember? It was the only time he'd ever been in such a rage!"

"Oh yes!" Ana began, "It was horrible but he missed you by a mile! And you *were* being awful and rude to mama, remember? You were scolding, mocking her for her overcooked asparagus!"

Joanna was irritated, "Oh come on, it was more than that; he was angry about something else!"

"What?" Dolores asked wide-eyed.

"Because he knew he loused up, you know, showing me off to his old friend, competing with him about who had produced the best child—but it all went haywire. Papa really didn't want me to go ahead and *marry* Tim, to leave!"

"So why did you?" Ana sighed, her large dark eyes glistening with tears. "I begged you not to leave us!"

"Not because he threw the chair but because of what he

said—"

"What? I don't remember," Dolores exclaimed.

Joanna was on the point of tears, "He said he **had** thought I was special, way beyond my age, but that he'd been wrong. He really hurt me. I'd always tried so hard. I'd even agreed to dating Tim in the first place though I hadn't wanted to."

"I knew it! I knew you didn't love him!" Ana said triumphantly, "Why didn't you leave him and come to England?"

"Yes, why didn't you, why don't you now?" Dolores asked.

"I don't know, he's not so bad, we're good friends, I just can't, I don't know why?"

"I know why you can't, won't," Ana murmured.

"Why?" Joanna asked stifling a sob.

"Because mama hasn't asked you to come home."

"What!" Joanna retorted irritably. "She doesn't matter to me at all, she never has, only papa—"

"You *do* care and she cares for you! She shut herself up in a room when we got settled in England. I knew it was because she was ashamed, ashamed of not having followed her instincts and stopping your marriage, at least trying!"

"I didn't know—" Joanna murmured.

At that moment Tomás returned saying they had to get going if they were to be back on the road, to their car, by dark.

Leaving the plateau they headed up a steep rocky path, the rain still falling but not as heavily. They didn't mind being cold and mud-splattered. They were looking forward to seeing the grand summit where a magnificent aperture would loom large and from which wisps of smoke would emerge and fly off into the sky like magical birds carrying special messages. Perhaps these messages were meant for them. But as they entered a heavy fog seeing very little in front of them Tomás told them they were already at the top. They couldn t believe it. Looking up at what was supposed to be the brink of the orifice all they saw was a flying mist leading to nothingness. Tomás quickly stretched his long arm across the path, "We can't go any further without falling right in!" After a moment he continued, "Be still, very still, listen!" The three sisters stood as quietly as possible in the white fog. Little by little they began to hear a low-toned deep-voiced groan, almost a growl. This was followed by a higher-pitched drawn out cooing coming straight towards them. They reached for each other's hands. They were at the edge of an unseen force, the unknown, perhaps the future or was it the past? They gripped each other's hands more tightly. At that moment they merely existed, having no age, shape or size; for that one moment the three sisters would have happily welcomed their father's stubby fingers, his square hands appearing out of nowhere and becoming part of the pulsating tangle of wet cold flesh. After all he was just another creature like themselves at the edge of nowhere.

In the end, towards the very end of that moment, but only for that moment, they would have also welcomed their mother's delicate slender fingers as she tremulously joined them.

SPOTTED ROSES

Joanna never got to her father's funeral in England after he died suddenly at the age of sixty-two. She had been far away in the Maya archaeological site of Chichen-Itza in Mexico holding an umbrella over her husband's head while he did stone rubbings in the hot sun. She wondered if that's what she'd been doing the moment her father died of a coronary thrombosis so long ago when she was in her late twenties. To this very day Joanna finds this thought to be very perturbing.

What had his life been like the whole last year before his death? Did something happen that contributed to this catastrophe of the body, a healthy body with no discernible disease? Perhaps it had been a catastrophe of the spirit also.

She pictured him and mama strolling on cobble stoned lanes, under arches in all the old towns in Devon, stopping once in awhile to drink tea. For him it would be strong black tea with a touch of heavy cream; for her, jasmine tea with a little sugar. They wouldn't have talked much. They never had. Benita might smile in her beguiling tranquil way addressing him as "*hijito*" which literally meant "little son" but was the equivalent of "sweetie," "honey" or "darling." He had often seemed to be her eldest child, her only son, always getting the best cuts of meat, second helpings of her strawberry shortcake. She monitored the household so that there was absolute silence whenever he slept, read his myriad newspapers or when he was merely tired or sad. Worrying about his spendthrift ways she stashed away some of the money he would give her for daily expenses. Then she and her three daughters would have to do without new clothes, shoes and sometimes even without medical and dental care. She took to making all their clothes. Joanna would never forget her embarrassment as a teenager having to wear a dress that looked like a plaid sack with a crisp white collar and white cuffs. But no matter how well Benita looked after him he would still have sat with her in the tea-shop in Devon looking like a lonely waif, small wrinkled bald, all hunched over.

What else happened during this last year? In the beginning of the year Keith and Benita had come to New York to celebrate Joanna's marriage to James (she had divorced Tim long before). It was a strange visit—too much drinking, words slipping out that were not meant to be formed in the first place. "We know what it is to love, don't we?" Keith had said to Joanna, his blue eyes twinkling with delight, smiling in that mischievous naughty way he reserved for his daughters knowing they'd go into their mock coquettish act, hugging him, kissing him first on both sides of his face and finally on his soft moist lips. But this time Joanna hadn't reacted in her usual way. After all she was married, passionately in love with a man who was only ten years younger than her father. As a matter of fact, she'd ignored his comment, only to later tell him something mean at the dinner table. It dismayed her not to remember what she had said because Keith had fainted, his head falling upon his plate of food, the few hairs on the top of his head looking limp, forlorn. To this day Joanna reproaches herself for having hurt him so deeply.

What else happened that year? He'd begun to write his memoir since he had just retired from Pan American Airways. He had first been a radioman, later airport manager during the company's first ventures into Latin America. He'd met Benita, sired his daughters all the while hankering after the life of a European gentleman and later on during the Spanish Civil War, as World War II approached, dreaming about the heroic life of an idealistic warrior. But in letters to Joanna he said he was so displeased with his writings, with his memoir, that day after day he'd torn up the previous day's work.

She imagined him squinting, no glint in his blue eyes, a cigarette dangling from his dry lips, his face full of tiny wrinkles with no space left for more.

Then his mother died of a heart attack in her eighties after a fall down a flight of stairs. Joanna had pictured him in a squashed hat, tall riding boots and an officer's army jacket looking for a spot to plant a rose bush in memory of his mother, Mary. He kept walking round and round the house unable to decide where to lay down the bundle of rose roots. Tears flowed, his nose ran while a drizzly fog followed his every step, finally thoroughly soaking him, leaking right through his hat onto his delicate scalp. He came to a stop at the back of the house called Rosedene—that was the address, no number, no street name. He decided the rosebush would be planted under his bedroom window overlooking the orchard on the sloping hill leading to Torbay where sailboats, yachts and fishing boats were moored, vessels ready to carry wandering souls to the ends of the world or even to bring them to Rosedene. Would the spirit of his mother Mary be coming to visit? Probably not. Keith hadn't lived with her since he was fourteen when he had run away from home becoming a hobo riding trains. He also hadn't lived with her for the first five years of his life. Unmarried she hadn't been able to care for him, temporarily leaving him with her married sister. Mary wasn't soft and loving, "never had the time," she had been fond of saying to her grandchildren adding "too busy putting bread and meat on the table." She was short, rotund, a little troll in print dresses, white stockings and black lace-up booties, her image making it difficult for anyone to imagine how she could ever have been young, been wooed, bedded and delivered of four flourishing lives. "My hands were meant for peeling potatoes, my feet for stomping through mud," she would have said. But would she now come to visit, to take her first born, her little Keith to her dead bosom, to soothe him, to tell him how much she loved him even though at the age of five he'd lost all his hair on the sea voyage to New York after she'd fetched him back from her sister's home in England. When the hair never grew back except in little spidery wisps, she knew it had to do with the shock of discovering that she was his real mother. She hated him for not immediately accepting her, for being endlessly surly and so she'd avenged herself by doting on her next son with his head of thick curls and his dimply smile.

Keith dug a deep hole double the length of the rose roots and tenderly he'd planted them hoping the roses would be pure white as the nursery promised. Before long the roses bloomed but they were not white, not *all* white. They were speckled, splattered with red spots. They turned their heads towards the bay, towards the vessels that were ready to transport those wishing to leave the town of Torquay, the house called Rosedene. Then there were the vessels that had just arrived bringing visitors. Perhaps not only Mary would be arriving. Perhaps Joanna would also be coming, coming with an umbrella to hold over papa's head protecting him from the falling mist, protecting him from the thought that anyone could take his place, not even her husband. But Joanna never arrived.

Keith died a few months later in his sleep, a blood clot rushing to his heart like a torn-off thorn that had been hidden by the bespeckled rose petals.

Bus Trip to Quintana Roo

It was hot and muggy in Merida, Yucatan as Joanna and her mother settled into the hard seats of the dusty bus. Joanna knew that her mother didn't want to be in her homeland Mexico, not even to visit her mother Zali in Chetumal, Quintana Roo.

"Don't expect Chetumal to be any prettier than the last time you saw it!"

"Stop worrying! I just need to get to know Abuela Zali a little bit better now that I'm older," Joanna answered, looking at her mother once again as discreetly as possible. Despite looking very much like the Maya men and women in the bus with her olive-brown skin, broad shoulders and short legs, she looked out of place. Against Joanna's wishes Benita had insisted on wearing a lace blouse, a grey-blue gabardine suit and tiny suede pumps with pom-poms on top.

"But why?"

"I don't know, I just need to," Joanna answered almost inaudibly, not wishing to let on that she needed to be with her mother, to know her better, perhaps through the eyes of her grandmother.

"Well, I find it strange; you've always been so disdainful of me," Benita exclaimed, her fingers nervously picking at her hair, trying to bolster up her unraveling French twist.

"So, why did you agree to come then?"

Looking out of her window Joanna's mother didn't answer right away; she seemed engrossed by the loading of enormous blocks of ice into the compartment below. Not even turning to look at her daughter, she murmured, "I was pleased you wanted to be with me."

As the bus got on its way with a strangulated roar she quickly added, "There's something I need to tell you, but not this moment—before we get there," and turning away from the window she closed her eyes, folding her arms over her round belly. Joanna was immediately alarmed; what secrets awaited her?

Benita continued, "As you know, abuela is the opposite of me, strong, tough—I've told you how she used to row across that treacherous Rio Hondo to British Honduras to buy groceries which she'd then sell to the community?"

"Yes, you told me!" Then, fearful that she sounded critical, Joanna added, "Tell me more about her, how did she get her name?"

"Her father Balam named her Quetzali, you know, after the beautiful bird."

"Balam! Did you know him?"

"No, he died when I was very little; all I remember is a voice going on and on in a strange language."

"Oh," Joanna said, knowing that her grandmother's side of the family was Maya.

"Mama Zali said he was a professional traveling story-teller. But, *mi hija*, let's not talk anymore; I need to rest."

"Yes, I do too," Joanna agreed, "we hardly slept last night. I heard you tossing and turning and whimpering a little when you finally fell asleep."

"And you were grinding your teeth; I didn't realize you still did that! You know you always did as a child, don't you?"

"Yes, you've told me," Joanna sighed. Then, tucking her full skirt between her legs and intertwining her ankles she closed her eyes.

When she awakened, the lush farmland had turned into prickly brush and the road was only a narrow path barely the width of the bus. There was an aroma of corn tortillas and refried beans in the air as the people around them quietly ate. Here and there she heard words she didn't understand, probably from one of the many Maya languages in the region. They might have been the only ones speaking Spanish.

"Are you awake Joancita?" Benita asked, gently touching her arm.

"Yes, I'm just now remembering a wonderful dream I was having! I dreamt that I was little, sleeping on this bus with my head on your chest!"

Benita squeezed her arm so hard it hurt. Then, stroking the imprint of her fingers she said, "What I have to tell you, I really don't *want* to tell you, but I must before we get to Zali's!"

Putting her hand on top of hers, Joanna mumbled, a little tremulously, "It's okay Mama, go ahead."

Almost in a whisper she told Joanna how she'd been forced to live with a Mexico City government official for a whole year when she was fourteen, that if Zali hadn't consented the whole town would have been severely punished.

"My God!" Joanna exclaimed, inadvertently pulling her arm away from her mother's touch, "How could she do such a thing? Did she fight for you when they came to get you? Did she scream?"

"No, she felt she had no choice, don't you see?"

And Benita gingerly returned her hand to Joanna's arm, "Sometimes people can't help what they do, even what they do to their own children."

Then, taking a long breath, she continued, "Why do you think I had to tell you this story?"

"So I'd see *Abuela* Zali with different eyes?"

Benita suddenly put her head on Joanna's shoulder clumsily trying to embrace her, sniffling a little as she whispered hoarsely, "I did something similar. I allowed you to marry when I knew you weren't in love. I allowed your father to steer you towards a marriage with the son of his old friend but worst of all I stood by helplessly, knowing you were challenging me, whether you knew it or not, challenging me to stop the whole thing! I almost died when we were transferred to England and we had to leave you behind! You were only seventeen and still such a child, a baby really!"

Joanna stiffened her whole body, a coldness suffusing her inside and out, "I almost died too!" she retorted with a harshness that surprised her, "only I didn't know why!"

"Please try to understand. I should have fought for you; I just couldn't!"

"Maybe you wanted to be rid of me!"

"No, how can you say that?" Benita cried, moving away and covering her face with her hands. Joanna remained stiff, unmoving. Then slowly uncovering her face, turning towards her daughter she continued, "Before I met your father I had three babies with a no-good man I loved."

She took a deep breath, "They all died, so you have *no* idea how I felt. Don't tell me I wanted to be rid of you."

"Were they girls?" Joanna asked coldly, staring straight ahead at all the dented sombreros and crowns of braids

"No, three boys with large black eyes, long lashes, petulant little mouths."

"What did they die of?"

"Bad food, bad milk, bad everything."

"How horrible!" Hesitantly she put her hand on her mother's thigh—so soft, yielding. "It's okay, mama. I got divorced anyway and I'm very happy with James now, so don't feel bad."

As the old bus approached Chetumal everyone sniffed a little, suffocated by the smell of human waste, of pig's blood from the slaughterhouse. At the barren depot passengers scattered in all directions, some turning to look at them quizzically. They walked four blocks on a dirt road passing cabins with tin roofs.

Suddenly ahead of them still in the distance they saw a tiny woman standing in the middle of the road. She was wearing a loose white dress with lace ruffles at the bodice and at the hem, a flowing lace headband across her forehead; dark brown flesh, the color of a hazelnut, a dazzling smile.

She walked forward nimbly on small sandaled feet, arms extended, ready to embrace them. Joanna was startled by the strength of her arms, the firmness of her back, the elastic silkiness of her cheeks. After all she was ten years older than the last time she'd seen her. Arm in arm, they entered her tiny courtyard, where a few scrawny chickens ran around a lopsided coop. Inside the one room hut was a square wooden table covered by a lace tablecloth, four wooden chairs with lace-covered cushions, a hammock and a sideboard cabinet, the top of it also covered by a lace mat.

The lace design was the same as that on her mother's blouse. She knew that Zali herself had crocheted all of the lace. She ran over and bending down she hugged her abuela so fervently her headband fell off. Before she could pick it up Zali hugged her back laughing raucously, "That's what I like, a little passion! It's so good to finally see you again.!"

Soon after Zali stepped into the courtyard and, grabbing a chicken, she wrung its neck. Joanna winced, turning away but then quickly turned back again. This time she was not disgusted. Benita was already lying down on the hammock. Zali motioned to Joanna to join her in the kitchen area. Placing the chicken on the counter she roughly plucked out its feathers.

"*Abuelita*, do you mind if I ask you questions?"

"No, *por supuesto* no—ask anything!"

Not able to ask what she really wanted to ask she said, "What was it like for you when your three grandchildren died?"

"How do you think I felt? One by one they went wasting away from fevers!"

"How did you get along with *your* mother?" Joanna continued, feeling awkward.

"I hardly knew her. Actually I didn't know her at all. She died shortly after I was born. Her name was Yia—it means Marigold. I had older siblings but they were all dead. Papa Balam and I were left all alone."

"Did you travel with him?"

"Oh yes! I learned all his stories, adding music to them, singing them, acting them out too!"

Then, as she singed the chicken's skin she continued, "I saw so much, beautiful things, bad things, fights, war, blood!" She cut the chicken into pieces and threw them into boiling water; into another pot of bubbling water she emptied a small sack of rice, "Fights between whites and Indians, Indians against Indians—so much blood!"

"No wonder Mama said you were strong, tough—what a life you must have had!"

"Dear *querida* Benita, she was fragile just like Mama Yia. I was so happy your Papa came along and saved her."

"If she was so fragile why did you give her away, sell her really when she was so young?"

Uncovering a bowl of previously cooked beans and pensively, slowly beginning to mash them, Zali answered, "So she finally told you. Good! I know she's never forgiven me and I'm truly sorry she suffered but I can't repent what was necessary."

"Yes, I understand what was at stake, but to throw her out of her home, to send her away from her family, to throw her to the wolves!"

"I know, I know—I had to harden myself to do it but I did it. I knew all about sacrifices, terrible ones ever since I was a baby."

"What do you mean? What sacrifices?" Joanna stepped closer to her little grandmother as she removed the bones from the boiled chicken, placing the chunks of meat into a spicy chocolate sauce that had been on the window sill.

"Don't be shocked but Balam and I were witnesses to many sacrificial ceremonies."

"Really?" Joanna exclaimed.

"Yes, we wanted our Gods to help us, to advise us, console us—I guess even to love us no matter what."

"And something had to be sacrificed?" Joanna's voice

trembled.

"Yes, chosen people had to pierce their cheeks, lips or tongue. Then they had to pass cloth strips right through the wound and then burn the bloodied offerings."

She gasped as Zali continued, "The Gods would take on a human shape, come to life in effect within the holy smoke."

"Oh, how painful! Surely *you* didn't have to do such things!"

Zali smiled. Then, turning to face Joanna she pulled down her lower lip, revealing a glaring red wound, a scar that was hidden from sight by her full pouting lower lip. Despite her shock Joanna was intrigued by the idea of a balance: to get something, you give something."

Suddenly Benita was with them, embracing them; Joanna hadn't even realized she'd awakened. Without having to be told what to do, Benita took out three enormous wooden plates and spoons and put the rice and beans on one side of the plate and the móle chicken on the other and handing the others their plates she led the way to the table where she'd already placed three wooden goblets filled with Mescal.

They ate and drank in silence, now and then smiling at one another. Finally Zali turned to Joanna, "In your own way did you ever make a sacrifice in order to get something?"

"Yes, I think so," Joanna answered immediately without thinking.

Zali smiled, "You don't have to tell what it is, what it was."

Joanna turned to look at her mother. She must have looked at her longingly, with a clear yearning, for she reached for one of her daughter's hands, brought it up to her face and stroked her own cheek with it. Smiling even more broadly Zali lifted her goblet, urging them to do the same, "*Arriba, Abajo, Al Centro, Adentro*, (Up, Down, To the Center, To the Inside!)"

After a short pause she added, "To the sky above, to the earth below, to our hearts!" Then in unison they drank the searing raw liquid relishing how it warmed their insides.

Looking for the Holy Woman

Lena's face was calming, soothing—heart-shaped, soulful slanted eyes with long thick lashes, tawny cheeks. It almost reduced Joanna's painful nostalgia. So when Lena suggested they go to Jamaica together, the home of her grandparents before they'd all immigrated to Oyster Bay Long Island, Joanna immediately consented.

Soon they were drinking Planter's Punch at an English pub in Montego Bay. Lena murmured, "Please forgive me for saying this; I've been meaning to, for a long time, but you've been looking so sad and distant; you only come alive when you're singing and dancing with your class, with your little ones."

"God! Has it been that obvious?" Joanna responded, feeling exposed.

Lena continued, "Why can't you go back to your husband and work things out? He loves you so very much, maybe too much but still—do you realize how great it is to be loved at all?"

"What makes you think he loves me?" Joanna asked in a low voice, pushing her long hair away from her face.

"The way he looks at you, so appreciative, of your every word. And look how he's always encouraging you to keep on studying, going back for more degrees even though it takes time away from him!"

"I know, I know, but then he gets those fits of jealousy, becoming so harsh, critical, accusing me of being unfaithful!"

"But why?" Lena was emphatic. "After all he's not crazy!"

"What do you mean?"

"Don't get upset but he *is* intelligent, sensitive. Have you ever

158

wondered what it is that makes him so insecure, what it is he senses about you?" Lena asked cautiously.

"Are you saying that he's right to behave the way he does, that there's something wrong with me?"

"No, no, not really, not actually, but could you be creating shadows of other presences that are getting between the two of you?"

Joanna squirmed around on her barstool, "I don't know what you're talking about! He just has a problem about women betraying him like his mother did; he told me all about it—how she French-kissed him till he was three and then dumped him out of guilt."

Lena didn't say anything more on the subject; she merely stroked Joanna's arm smiling affectionately. Lena had never before been so forward and she had yet to talk of her own life. There were rumors among the school staff that she'd been a runaway teenager, an exotic dancer and a mistress to Joe Louis, the famous boxer.

"You know Lena, you can be awfully spooky sometimes, it frightens me! My creating specters and all that!" Joanna murmured.

"Well, talking of specters, there's two guys across from us who have been watching us since we arrived. They're kind of nice, what do you think?"

"Look, I didn't come here to get laid!" Joanna retorted irritably, glancing quickly at the men noting they were attractive, well-groomed and around their age, in their middle thirties. "Tell me more about what you were saying, about those shadows, presences, whatever, that I dredge up to louse up my marriage!"

"I'm sorry. I guess I'm just affected by being here in my homeland. I heard a lot of stories from my grandmothers about spirits from the mountains who were always hunting for a place they could call home, you know, some kind of unsuspecting soul. She called them Los Secrétos."

"Secrétos! How strange—secrets, just plain secrets?"

"Yes," was all Lena answered.

As soon as some barstools around them were vacated the two men sauntered over and introduced themselves. The tall dark-haired one called Mark came to sit by Joanna's side, while Bruce, a blonde, somewhat shorter than Mark, sat on the other side of Lena. Both wore trim sports jackets, ascots and spoke like upper class Britons.

"What were you girls talking about? You looked so charmingly engrossed," Mark asked.

"Oh this and that, our dark side," Joanna replied coquettishly as Lena glanced at her with surprise.

"Well, you've come to the right place. We hear there are spiritualists up in the mountains who can tell you all about the fiends that creep, slither, hop and fly!"

"I'd love to meet a real witch!" Joanna laughed, while Mark and Bruce looked at each other nodding their heads as if to say, "We'll see what we can do about that!" Again Lena looked at Joanna unbelievingly poking her slightly with her elbow. Joanna poked her back indicating that she shouldn't worry, that she was okay about the men.

Soon the four of them were in a cabaret. Besides being hungry, they wanted to hear some native music. They were disappointed when they saw that there were empty tables only at the back of the room. Before Lena and Joanna could protest Mark and Bruce had lifted up some small tables and chairs and had carried them way up to the front, next to the stage, in front of everyone else. No one said anything or tried to stop them. After the show and snacks of tiny meat pies and sweet fruits, they danced to drums most of the night. At dawn Mark and Bruce took them back to their hotel, leaving them at their door after arranging to pick them up in the afternoon to go looking for Maga-the-Hag, the spiritualist living high up in the wild hills.

As Mark drove them up the mountain with Joanna at his side, she felt more relaxed than she'd felt in a very long time. The four of them had blended together so well. It surprised her how easily she and Mark had gravitated towards each other. Was it because she was so heartsick? Or was she avenging herself for being called "unfaithful" for so long? Or could it be she was simply attracted to Mark despite his elegant genteel arrogance or who knows perhaps *because* of it? But why should she need to feel like this, almost like a child needing a strong, protective presence? She thought it made her feel a part of a bigger power. Once again she found it difficult to know what she was feeling. Why? Why? Now that's a question she could put to Maga-the-Hag who was purported to have a gift for divining people's most hidden thoughts, feelings.

"You know," Joanna began enthusiastically, "I had a sort of witch in our family but she was called a Healer; she was our grandmother's sister-in-law, Balita, from the Yucatan. Her only child died in his youth; she wanted to die also but as she was about to ingest a poison of her own making it occurred to her that if she could create a substance that kills why not one that heals!"

"Yes, long ago I had one too in my family," Lena said tapping Joanna knowingly on her back. "Mine was from around here somewhere. I never knew her, just heard about her. She was called the Eye Witch; she was like the owl who never looked at the sun."

"Balita wasn't *magical*!" Joanna interrupted, "She could only soothe and heal with her herbs, making medicine out of water, making it seethe bubble and rise up. She could remove growths within the body without cutting, chopping and all that blood."

"I'm not trying to outdo you!" Lena chuckled leaning forward from the back seat and embracing Joanna's shoulders, "But my Eye Witch could get people suffering from all kinds of love obstructions to open up, revealing the roots of their pain."

"How on earth did she do that?" queried Bruce moving closer to Lena.

"Simple," Lena declared putting her head on Bruce's shoulder, "She'd kill an owl, remove its heart and place it on the sick person's

161

left breast whereupon she was able to see, to feel Los Secretos, their hidden secrets."

Joanna persisted, "I know these are only stories but one last thing about Balita—she wasn't so theatrical; it cost her dearly to do her healing; the more good she did the more she was diminished. She understood that the love for others both gives and takes away one's own life. Don't you see, it's a transaction undertaken only by the brave and those with faith!"

"Hey there," Mark began, tenderly stroking Joanna's thigh, "Why so serious all of a sudden; what's going on in that lovely head of yours?"

Lena laughed, "My Eye Witch was more human; she wouldn't let herself be diminished! Her spirit lives on forever and ever in butterflies!"

"Butterflies?" they all exclaimed together.

"Well not just any butterfly but the Owl Butterfly, the one with a great eye imprinted upon each wing to ward off predators."

"Lena, Lena," Bruce chucked, "Look how warm you've become, almost feverish; are you sure your ancestor didn't pass on her powers to you!"

Eventually they found the home of Maga-the Hag, a thatch-roof hut half buried by giant plants with green leaves striped in red and covered by a multitude of dwarf flowers merged together suffocating each other. Frogs of all sizes hopped around everywhere, all around them and beyond, but Maga was not to be found. Maybe she was one of the frogs, already working her art of divination upon them.

"Well, it's clear," Bruce shouted, "The deep inner message is that we must go and make our own magic!"

Lena and Joanna knew without discussing it that they were going to end up in the men's hotel high up on one of the hills overlooking the town. A butler met them at the front door of their enormous suite. A maid escorted Lena and Joanna to a peach-colored marble bathroom to wash up and even change, if they wanted, into one of the silk caftans hanging on the hooks. Later, servants served them a dinner of caviar, a delicate seafood soup, rare prime ribs of beef, Yorkshire pudding and a vast variety of spicy cooked and raw vegetables. The wines were plentiful. After the table was cleared the servants disappeared. They danced slowly, quietly as if they were under a spell. Then eventually each couple disappeared into a bedroom.

Mark and Joanna began to kiss each other as soon as they had closed the door, their mouths becoming silky, aromatic, melting together. Then Joanna fainted. Was it because she wished Mark was her husband James? When she came to, they were naked and in bed, drenched in their blended sweat and sensual secretions, Mark on top and inside of her. His usual plastered down hair was ruffled up in every direction, mascara all over his face rendering him the look of an Indian on the warpath, his yell that of a victorious warrior, Joanna's the moan of a vanquished foe who'd lost not only her hair but her head. What on earth had been going on, in her deeper consciousness, in her world of primitive images during the time she had blacked out? She couldn't even guess at what it was but she knew with all her heart that in the near future she had to try to find out. She knew that she must, that she would return to her husband. She missed him with all of her being.

After they'd rested, bathed, the four of them emerged from the bedrooms one by one, naked, all looking as if they were under a spell. They glided into the veranda and silently stretched out on the enormous couch on their stomachs and fell asleep, ending up all in a row surrounded by pillows of every size and color but all striped in red. Joanna was the first to awaken the next morning right before the dawn. She raised her head and looked around. The lights of the town were still shining, the ragged-edged half-moon beginning to dim. She smiled as she gazed at all their bare buttocks lying side-by-side so peacefully, so innocently. Then she thought she saw something on one of Lena's cheeks but she wasn't sure, maybe she was seeing things. She blinked several times focusing intently. Yes, there on one of Lena's taut olive-brown buttocks was a tattoo of an Owl Butterfly, it's magnificent golden eyes already beginning to gleam in the first light of day.

A TRIP TO DIE FOR

What an ordeal it had already been, navigating an eighty-seven year old man in a wheelchair from New York City to the ancient walled city of Tulum on the Quintana Roo coast, on the Mexican Caribbean. But as the little tour train approached the entrance Joanna gasped with dismay for there, at the foot of the gate to the walls, lay a set of steep crumbling steps. No one had said anything about them.

The Cruise Director had mentioned there was no hydraulic lift on the bus taking them from the pier to the train, that her husband would have to be manually lifted on and off the bus. They had mentioned there was a short train ride from the final bus stop to the ruins. She had also known that even getting from the ship to the ferry would be back breaking because of the heavily ridged, swaying ramp. Equally daunting information had been that the wheelchair wouldn't fit through the doorway to their stateroom so that as it turned out their Home Health Aide, who was traveling with them, would have to lift James out off his wheelchair, place his frail arms around his own strong neck and face-to-face walk backwards into the room holding the ravaged body by the waist as if they were doing a slow dance. Even negotiating the transfer from the wheelchair to the gurney in the airplane itself so as to move up and down the aisles to their seats had not been easy but it had been at least a matter of strength and knowledge of body mechanics on the part of the aide.

So, especially after having surmounted so many obstacles, the impediment of the ancient steps left them deeply disappointed.

A few weeks after the trip, as Joanna thought about the trip, her husband cried out in pain from the bedroom. He was only being washed by their faithful aide, but James's skin, muscles and bones could no longer endure the slightest human touch, yearning to be left alone to merge with the ultimate, non-intrusive quiet of infinity.

At the time they had planned this trip they were only thinking of how they could get out of their Manhattan apartment to give James a change from merely lying in their king-size bed in their yellow bedroom. At first they had thought of renting a car and observing autumn in New England. Then when that seemed too pedestrian, they considered a week-end cruise to Bermuda leaving from a nearby westside dock. But because of the onset of winter there was only one more scheduled cruise and it was totally booked.

However, there were plenty of cruises leaving from Miami which they hadn't considered because the problems of flying at high altitude with James's congestive heart failure necessitating a precautionary oxygen tank prescribed by his physician.

Foolhardy as it may seem they ended up booking an upper level stateroom with a private verandah on a popular ship sailing from Miami to Key West and on to the Mexican Island of Cozumel.

Trying to overcome their disappointment at the unexpected flight of steps to the Temples they devised a plan. At least two members of their trio would take turns visiting the temples above, taking photos and preparing verbal descriptions for James's vicarious pleasure.

The aide went first, leaving them in the hot sun for there was no shade anywhere. A woman vendor offered an enormous straw hat to protect James's delicate pink baldness appearing above his long white hair and beard. He refused, wanting to feel the sun upon his head.

As they drank a little of their warm bottled water they chatted about how good it was to have come even this close to the temples, how fortunate they had been to have seen the other

Maya ruins at Chichén-Itzá and Uxmal when they were younger and healthier and had gotten permission to do stone rubbings of the bas reliefs because James was an artist as well as an aficionado of archaeology.

After the passage of perhaps a quarter of an hour, three small Mexicans in khaki Bermuda shorts and matching shirts approached them, asking in broken English if they wanted to see the ruins. Joanna explained their predicament in Spanish. After listening to Joanna quietly, one of the three asked again if they wanted to see the ruins, that they could lift the wheelchair. Joanna answered emphatically "yes!" and "how much?" They answered that since they were Government Archaeological Guides there was no charge.

With great care and a surprising strength they lifted the wheelchair with James in it all the way up the gateway in what seemed like one gliding movement. One of the guides stayed with them to push the wheelchair and show them around. Before long their aide joined them overjoyed they had miraculously made it upwards.

The grassy terrain was rocky and bumpy but the warm breezes descending from the vast blue sky and the Caribbean Sea nearby gently swayed the palm trees scattered here and there among the temples.

There are few joys that can compare with what Joanna felt seeing "her tattered lion," as she affectionately called her husband, visiting the ruins of a grandness long gone, of carved, winged, descending Gods who represented the setting sun, of elegantly robed, masked, painted and bejeweled priests presiding over all that is earthly as well as all that is ethereal. Ironically, they knew these carvings and frescoes were there though they couldn't come anywhere close to them. They too needed to be protected against human touch.

It was all a memorial as well as a eulogy to her dear husband without his having to be dead to receive it.

THE BROWN BOY FROM BRAZIL

It was hot in the town of Oaxaca. Joanna sat down to rest in the tiled corridor surrounding the courtyard of the Museo de Arte Prehistorico to which Rufino Tamayo had donated his whole collection of Pre-Colombian art. Still savoring her pleasure in having seen all the Olmec statues, the ones with the fierce yet babyish looking faces, (the ancestors of her Maya mother), she noticed someone looking at her from across the courtyard, a long slender bell-shaped person in tones of black and brown, half-hidden behind a pillar. Then when she looked again there was nobody there. A little later a block away she discovered that the curb was so steep she'd never be able to climb down. No problem—she would just find a better curb. Suddenly a voice spoke right behind her, close by, in English but with a slight Spanish accent.

"May I help you, señora?"

Turning around she saw a tall brown boy in black bell-bottom trousers tapering upward to a slender waist and a long but softly muscular chest in a black t-shirt. Maybe he was fourteen or fifteen.

"May I help you? I'm very strong."

Joanna laughed knowing she was too heavy for him but she was enchanted by his sparkling green eyes, his curly eyelashes, rosy cheeks and his Afro.

"No one realizes how big and strong I am. I can do anything I want if I think about it with all of my mind!"

Before long, as they walked looking for a good curb, she found out he was in a work-study program, that his mother was a flamenco dancer, his father a sculptor who worked with wood and that they had adopted him in Brazil. Hiring him as her guide they decided to go to the Zapotec archaeological site of Monte Alban the very next day.

As they began to climb upwards from the taxi parking space to the ruins, Náes asked her to lean on his shoulders—how solid his slender neck, shoulders and back felt! Finally stopping to rest on a wooden bench that had been built around a huge multi-trunked cypress tree, Náes asked, "What work do you do?"

"I used to be a psychotherapist until my husband became very ill and I needed, well, I wanted to look after him."

"He died, yes?"

"Yes, so now I write stories."

"About what?"

"Life, people I've known, myself."

"Why?"

"Why what?"

"Why write?"

"To understand, to try to have others understand who I am." Seeing his intensely quizzical look she added, "I guess it's hard for you to understand that even older people like me, who can hardly walk struggle with trying to figure out who they are!"

"Oh, I already know all that! I know who *I* am, so when I'm old like you, I'll still know!"

Chuckling, Joanna asked him to tell her more about himself.

"I'm Náes from Brazil. I live here with all the farms, orchards and wild places. My mother is beautiful with long silky black hair. I help my father with his statues by finding things to put on them, pebbles, feathers, egg shells, bird claws, lizard tails, even cat teeth. I've been looking for eyes but they're all too squashed up when I find them! I work as a Guide with people from all over the world and I'm learning many languages!"

Then, tearing at the bark of the giant tree he added, "See, I know who I am. So I don't have to write."

As he spoke she noticed that his face twitched now and then, shadows from the swaying leaves above him seemed to move his features, sometimes blackening the area around his eyes, splitting his full lips in two, making one side of his face higher than the other.

Soon they began walking again, this time in a barren dry open area with temples scattered here and there in the distance. Joanna was entranced by the tomb of a king depicted as a warrior with a skull face who had been buried with all his live servants around 1400. As gruesome as the idea was, she could almost relish the thought of this ultimate sacrifice to honor a loved one. (Of course in this case the servants had no choice).

"You know, señora, you should come back to Oaxaca on November 1, the Day of the Dead! You see photos of dead people surrounded by huge orange flowers and little pumpkins, chocolates and little white sugar skulls with the names of those who have been left behind written right on them! You know, the names of all those who have been abandoned!"

She felt like embracing the boy—yes it's true, when someone dies it's as if they have abandoned you.

Finally they were standing in front of a series of bas reliefs called The Dancers.

"They're not dancers; it's a bad name. You see how twisted they look, contorted? They're hunchbacks, pregnant women giving birth and people who can't walk!"

"Like me?"

Ignoring her Náes continued with fervor, "They all have special powers, great powers."

"What kind of power?" Joanna asked.

"A special power because they can't hide; they can't pretend to be different, so they are good. Like you—you wobble around like you're falling but you keep moving forward."

Tears filled her eyes. She felt both insulted and yet incredibly flattered—if only it were true, the part about moving forward.

When they said goodbye at the end of her visit she had the uncanny feeling that not only had she always known him but that they would meet again.

* * *

On the day of the dead, November first of the same year, Joanna went to visit the Maya archaeological site in Palenque. As she headed for the steps that led to the plateau of temples, she wondered if she should have talked to Náes further about his life, his family. She missed him; perhaps he could have come with her to Chiapas. Creeping up to the ruins, practically on all fours, chuckling to herself, she knew she might actually resemble the creature she'd come to see, the Waterlily Monster, who was on a bas relief on one of the temple portals. Upon reaching the plateau at the top of the steps she entered an immense misty deep green forest with temples not only among the trees but also perched far above, in the hills. It was a place for singing but not remembering the words of any song she merely hummed to the rhythm of the wind, vibrating atop the trees.

Looking up at The Temple of Inscriptions, unable to climb up its steep steps, Joanna could enjoy the lush green moss, the orange-colored lichen upon the stonework, the ferns that spilled out of the crevices. She knew that once, long ago, King Pacal's sarcophagus had been in that temple and that the sides of his tomb told his life story ending with his fall down the trunk of The Tree of the World into the open jaws of the Otherworld, accompanied by the half-skeletal demon carrying a bowl of blood that would one day reincarnate him. The sarcophagus also told the story of his son, Chan-Baklum and his ascension to the vacated throne; standing naked on the altar he pierced his penis three times with an obsidian knife. He then pulled long strands of bark paper through the wounds, immediately burning the paper so as to produce the smoke from which his Guide-God would emerge, ready to help him assume his father's throne. Chan-Baklum's eyes must have bulged, his mouth opened, his tongue hung out, as he mutilated himself, expressing anger, frustration and agony; anger that he had to suffer in order to please the powers that be; frustration that to become powerful he had to render himself powerless, even if only for a short time. He must have both loved and hated his father.

A little later Joanna crossed a stream and approached a steep path leading to the three temples Chan-Baklum had built to celebrate his enthronement, to celebrate himself and his Gods. He had earned the right. Had she built her own Temple through her work as a teacher, a guidance counselor, a psychotherapist? Through her joy, pain and struggle for almost forty years to love and to be loved by her husband James, even through his long illness, right up to his death?

Walking up the path to the portal of the temple she had come to see, she could almost see herself from above, as if she were being watched, a hulking figure in black and green, a kind of a foliage demon. Finally, there it was, The World Tree telling its story: the birth of the Waterlily Monster, its growth, its becoming the mother of bountiful ears of corn, its being rewarded by becoming transformed into a Celestial Bird, sitting up high, in the crown of the tree, overlooking the whole world.

Murmurings were coming from inside of the temple. As she approached the sounds she heard two male voices speaking in English, one beseeching, one resistive.

"You know I love you; I've loved you from the very beginning. You know that, don't you?"

"No, I don't!"

"Don't be like that! You know we belong together- we only have each other."

"I don't belong to anyone!"

"Yes, you do; I take care of you, haven't I always?"

"Get away from me, I don't need you!"

Then there was a short silence, a scuttling noise, a yell, loud and clear, "Let go of me, keep your hands off me!"

My God, it was Náes; it was his voice. Joanna rushed into the inner chamber of the temple, "Let go of him!" she shouted, seeing a robust man with gray hair trying to embrace the boy.

"Where the hell did you come from?," the man exclaimed, letting go of Náes, "Look lady, this is private business between myself and my son."

"Your son? Náes, are you okay?"

"Yes, señora, I'm fine," he answered not surprised in the least to see her, "He's my foster father and he wants to take me back to New York and I don't want to live with him anymore!"

For a few moments the three of them just stood there looking at each other. Then the man stepped towards Joanna extending his hand, "I'm Michael Garrity, and you are—?

"Akná," she answered, without thinking, inadvertently using her mother's pet name given to her by her mother. As she shook Michael's hand she noticed that despite the roughness of his skin and the strength of his fingers, he had a gentle warm grip.

"Oh, the mother of them all, the moon goddess!"

"How do you know—?"

"Oh, Mexico is my second home; I love this country but I need to get Náes back to school in the states and he keeps running away."

She glanced at Náes who only stared straight down at the stone floor, shrugging his shoulders, tears in his eyes, "I don't need him, I can take care of myself!"

"But you're still underage!" Joanna began trying not to think of what she had thought was happening between Michael and Náes when she had first heard their voices.

"I don't care! I just want to do what I want, not go to a stupid school!"

Looking briefly at Michael she said, "Forgive me but I have to ask, Náes is anyone doing anything to you that they shouldn't?"

As Michael shook his head, shocked, Náes answered, "He

treats me like a baby; I hate it! Can I live with you, señora? I can help you; I can travel with you; you need me!"

She was stunned. Náes must have been following her all along. Was he the spirit of her dead father, the little bald hobo, of his friend Earl, the lost poet, of James searching for a perfect love? What on earth could she say to the boy, only that he already had a parent? What could she do but embrace him knowing he would always be with her.

REUNION IN CHIAPAS

It was December and Joanna was in San Cristobal de Las Casas in Chiapas, Mexico, high up in the Sierra Madre mountains. Everywhere she looked, up and down hilly cobble-stoned streets, in the cafés around the village square, she thought she saw the shadow of Naés disappearing around a corner. She couldn't get the brown boy from Brazil out of her mind. Would he run away from his foster-father once again? Or could he be back in school in the states? Joanna had tried staying in touch but her letters had all been returned

She hoped he really wasn't in Chiapas; there was so much unrest, so much hostility between Zapatistas and the military. The new president held little hope for a resolution thus far since he hadn't even identified the plight of indigenous people as one of his new challenges.

Walking through the lush garden area of the village square, the park, she headed for the café housed in a gazebo-like structure right in the middle of the square. Vendors were all around, trays hanging from their necks full of candy, toys, and beautiful woven belts with diverse intricate patterns. As she approached the café she saw a sign in Spanish announcing a special reunion of foreigners who'd been deported from Mexico during the last six years since the Zapatista uprising of January 01 '94. It was a local government sign announcing their new approach of tolerance for foreigners previously accused of being Zapatista sympathizers, in the hope that all would understand how deeply the new local government wanted reconciliation and peace.

Joanna stared at the twenty or so persons seated at various

tables or walking around the cupola which contained a bar and a buffet table where a band would usually be. Everyone was drinking, eating, talking loudly in English. Seeing her, a short legged, bald man with long arms and a strong chest beckoned to her to join them.

"Come on in! You look like one of us!" And as he led her inside by the elbow, he continued, "I'm Bob Rich from Utah."

"I'm Joanna, a writer from New York City," she answered, feeling silly.

Bob led her to a woman with slanted eyes, some gray streaking her black hair.

"Joanna, meet Aura, a journalist from Argentina. Wait till you hear her story about Commander Ramona back in '96!"

Aura took a few steps towards Bob as if to playfully hit him.

She laughed, "Here I've been working all my life as a writer and now I'm only known as the chronicler of Ramona!"

"Oh," began Joanna, "I guess I can't ask you about her, though I'd love to!"

"Oh, I'm only kidding. I loved her. It's a sad story, though. She was so tiny in her embroidered blouse, her indigo skirt, her combat boots and her black ski mask and of all the luck she was dying of kidney cancer. What gorgeous eyes she had, but oh so frightened!"

As Bob backed off into the bustling crowd, Joanna asked, "How did you come to meet her?"

"I was covering the Indian Conference in Mexico City in '96, so I came here to Chiapas to talk to some of the Zapatistas who would be attending. The government was allowing Ramona and others to go as long as no one was armed."

"And she could travel being so sick?"

"Well, it was rough. We rode in a sports utility vehicle to the Pacific coast, her escorts on horseback; a government plane then took us all to Mexico City."

"What happened to her? Did she make a speech?"

"She couldn't even speak, much less walk, by the time we got there. She couldn't even get back. She died a few days later." Aura lowered her head for a moment, and then excused herself, saying she had to speak to someone who had just arrived.

Joanna began to walk in an aimless way, feeling awkward. Would she ever have been able to be as brave as Ramona. Cringing a little around the shoulders Joanna remembered an incident when she was in high school. The father of a friend knocked his daughter down in anger and Joanna said calmly, "That's not fair; you're bigger than she is." That's all she had been able to do or say. Her friend had later mocked Joanna's manner, her voice, her genteel words.

Wanting to distract herself Joanna approached a man in a voluminous, brown, hooded cassock, a large cross resting on his big belly. Seeing Joanna's approach, a pale, extremely serious-looking man who had been talking to the priest, walked away.

"I'm sorry to interrupt but I'm so drawn to your cross, the filigree work, is it French?" Joanna asked timidly.

"Yes, Father Michel Henri Jean Chanteau gave it to me; he wanted to be here but it was impossible. You know who he is, no?"

"Was he the priest who was expelled?"

"Yes, February of '98 and he'd lived and worked here for thirty-two years. To this day he feels like a Mexican. He still hasn't adjusted to being back in France!"

"Had he helped the Zapatistas?"

"Oh no, he refused to side with either the government or the rebels!"

"Then what happened? "

"Remember that massacre in December '97? His parish was in Chenalhó where the massacre occurred, the victims were his closest collaborators, they were members of an Indian Catholic Pacifist group who were constantly criticizing the federal and local governments for not caring for Indians but they hated the use of violence. Father Michel always said he preferred the gospel of St. Mark to the gospel of Subcommander Marcos, the Zapatista leader! But when he declared loudly that the rebels were not responsible for the massacre, and that a paramilitary group was; that was his undoing."

Joanna didn't know what to say. The priest soon slipped away, leaving her alone. Looking around, she saw that the pale, extremely serious-looking man who had been talking to the priest as she had approached, was now also alone. She was intrigued by his sensitive, deeply pensive face.

"Hello! I'm Joanna; I kind of crashed this event but I'm a writer from New York City."

Smiling shyly he answered, "I'm Ryan, a free-lance writer from the west coast, U.S.A. in a way we've all crashed this party called Chiapas!"

Joanna laughed a little, instantly liking him, "What aspects have you written about?"

"Well, I guess about the peace talks between the government and the Zapatistas. You know they collapsed September '96. Anyway, after a long time of not getting anywhere, in the Spring '99, 5,000 masked Zapatistas propagated their peace proposals across the country and organized balloting in every county in Mexico so everybody could express what they wanted'"

"How marvelous!" Joanna exclaimed.

"And listen to this! One noontime, during all the balloting, six masked rebels had lunch in the restaurant Sanborn in Mexico City and sat at the *very* same table where fighters in broad sombreros who followed Emiliano Zapata had eaten, *back* in 1914,"

"Fantastic! But what do *you* think should be done?"

"Well, it's very simple! The big landowners, all Spanish descendents and part of the government, will just have to learn how to share!"

Overhearing these words, a striking brown skinned woman with short white hair, strode over to them, her large brown eyes flaring with indignation. "That'll be the day! The powerful ones don't even *see* the Indians as human beings, how can they share their wealth with what they see as mere beasts! Even when the Indians do something really creative, beautiful, they're not recognized. Two years ago I was in Taniperla where I'd come to teach the villagers how to paint murals on the walls of their adobe town council buildings. When troops marched in May '98 the first thing they were ordered to do by the town leaders, the property owners, was to destroy the murals!"

A tall engaging-looking man with twinkly eyes, a constant smile on his face revealing unusually small teeth, spoke up, "Hello everyone! I couldn't help overhearing. Though I don't like defending the powers that be, I must say, they at least let Nettie Wild make her documentary film *A Place Called Chiapas*. She made it between June '96 and February '97, with help of course. We covered the story of the actual rebellion when the Zapatistas took over four towns, five-hundred ranches, all in the one week that it lasted. Anyway our film gives a great portrait of Marcos who'd been working for the Indian cause for twelve whole years. What a man! He talks in poetic metaphors, he leaves cryptic messages on the Internet. He bridges two worlds, that of a Spanish descendent and that of the Indian."

"What inspires someone who's so comfortably off to give up so much and go to live in the jungle, in muddy small towns to teach, to train?" asked Joanna of no one in particular. Then without waiting for an answer she continued, "I so admire anyone who is so committed, who knows so clearly what his mission in life is! Who is able to fight for what he wants."

The artist Amana looked at Joanna searchingly, warmly, her enormous eyes getting even larger.

"What do you do?"

"Well first I was a model, then a teacher, a guidance counselor, then a psychotherapist and now I am a fiction writer."

"I see you went from a passive object, to a useful one and

finally to creating your own objects, yes?"

"Yes," Joanna answered in a low voice.

Amana put a hand on one of Joanna's shoulders very briefly. Removing her touch she said, "Some people know their destiny early and for others it takes a whole lifetime. I guess it doesn't matter as long as you die knowing!"

"Hey, who's dying around here?" and Bob Rich joined the group.

"No one, don't worry," Joanna began, not wanting to explain, wishing to change the subject. "How on earth did you end up in Chiapas?"

"Simple! I buy coffee from Indian co-ops and market it for them, also their weavings. Now, what bothered the authorities was that I also made video documentaries and then I produced them through the web site. As they deported me the government told me, 'If you want to see Indians, see them in the markets or in the museums!'"

"Did you say you produced videos on Indian life, on the Zapatistas? "

"Yup! I've also helped local experts link all the civilian Zapatista committees all over Mexico through the Internet. We have a CD-Rom format, we have discs; anyone can visit with the Zapatistas in their stronghold, even in the jungle via computer. This is getting to be a high tech battle!" After a short pause, he continued, "We're also constantly training youngsters. There's one young kid, maybe he's fourteen, fifteen, who's taken to it all so brilliantly. He keeps repeating what Marcos once said in a speech, that what bothers the government the most was words, words of opposition. I must say, it's certainly true. Words are the rebels' best weapon and by continuing to speak up, loudly, persistently, they are doing their best fighting. But to return to this kid; there's something a little scary about him; he insists that when speaking fails, deadly weapons, guns, must be used!"

Joanna's body froze, a chill running from head to toe.

"What's the boy's name?"

"I don't know; we all call him Kid. Wait, once he told me his name; Nyce, you know like the bank system or Nice, like sweet."

"When did you meet him?"

"Way back in May. I found him in the muddiest town in the world, La Realidad, translating for some foreigners, escorting them from town to town. He told me he was an orphan and was totally on his own and liked it that way."

"Where is he? "

"Do you know this boy? He's somewhere in the Lacandón jungle in a training camp."

"Training? For what?"

"Obviously for war, if it becomes necessary. Ask Ryan, he knows where the camp is. I don't see him around; he must have gone back to his hotel, Diego de Mazariego. Do you know the Kid?"

Without answering, moving as quickly as she could, Joanna left the Café, heading back to her hotel, the same one Ryan was in.

What should she do now? Go to the Lacandón looking for Naés? Even if she made it, even if she found him, what then? Take him back with her to New York? Probably an impossibility, even if he wanted to leave.

Her whole body aching, her steps getting slower and slower, Joanna sat down on one of the park benches. Sighing deeply, she murmured softly:

"That is who I am, that is my destiny, to be a writer of words, words which will be forever, until the end, trying to break that clamor of muteness within me."

Joanna rose from the bench and headed for the hotel. Then suddenly, she once again thought she saw Naés' fleeting shadow. Would she ever see him again? Somehow she knew she would. She didn't know where, she didn't know when, but she would see him again.

TAÍNO WEDDING

Joanna needed help in caring for James at home in what turned out to be the last six months of his life. Many nurses' aides had to be rejected because they either couldn't be alone with a male patient, were prohibited from entering a kitchen by their tribal religion or just didn't want to do diapers. Finally Eliseo showed up at her door and she knew she could entrust her husband of so many years to him. How did she know this? Was it the way he looked, dressed all in white, tall, strong, swarthy, slanted black eyes, black hair brushed back into a ponytail? Perhaps. But also he could almost have been a long-lost relative on her Mexican mother's side of the family appearing just at the right time. Yes, that too. Or was it his expression, his audacious smile? For a split second she had thought he could be a long-lost son miraculously sired by a phantom lover of long ago, a son with an alluring blend of the nurturing and the picaresque, the feminine and the masculine, ethereal, yet infernal.

After James's death, Eliseo disappeared not even collecting his last week's salary. Then two years later he'd called to invite her to his house-warming party in the Bronx, saying he'd meet her at the subway station. He had waited for her behind a fluttering, flapping curtain of wings as he fed myriads of pigeons. He pointed out the first floor windows of his apartment as they approached his building. All she could see were tropical plants encircling the glass panes, twisting, bending, raising themselves towards the diminishing light, perhaps wanting to escape through the closed windows.

That evening Eliseo's living room had become a whirl of

movement as approximately ten people danced to Latin-American music, not as couples but as a group. Joanna didn't know who belonged with whom. There was the slender man with his upper lip lifting upwards in one corner. Had he arrived with the pretty woman with black hair cascading down to her waist, the one who had later removed her wig and falsies revealing herself to be a pretty boy? Did the professorial-looking man with the goatee belong with the plump woman with no makeup? And the woman with the raucous voice, did she belong with the wisp of a man with no expression on his face? Perhaps a few belonged to no one like Joanna, an older woman, and Eliseo in his mid-fifties.

After everyone had left he and Joanna strolled to a nearby park to clear their heads before he walked her to the taxi-stand. As they stood in front of the dolphin fountain he picked her up and placed her into the water as if it were a bassinette. As she sat laughing and splashing around, looking at his face, she saw something she hadn't seen before, his eyes had narrowed even more, a fierceness blazed through the slits, his lips were pressed tightly together as if he were trying not to snarl. But before she had time to be afraid he laughed and helped her out of the pond.

However, many months later when he told Joanna he was in trouble she wasn't surprised. He told her that after James's death, which had hit him as hard as his own father's and mother's death, he had returned to using heavy drugs. He had just signed up for an intensive rehabilitation program, beginning with detoxification. Would she stay with him that night to make certain he got to the hospital early the next morning? That night he had been like a large infant knowing nothing but hunger, thirst, and gratitude, "Hold me, touch me, kiss me as if I'm dying, the way you did with your husband." By the end of the night they had merged body and spirit, enjoying the architecture, transformations, the aromas of their deepest selves.

By the time they traveled to the mountains of Puerto Rico, many months later, to attend a wedding of two of Eliseo's oldest friends, they were a couple but neither one of them could have explained why. They were so different and not just in age. Yet she still had an uncanny feeling she had always known him. Perhaps it was the same with him. After hours of driving on a winding road full of bamboo trees torn asunder by hurricanes, thunderous rampaging waterfalls emerging like apparitions from steep walls of stone, they arrived at the farmhouse where the ceremony was to be held in the traditional manner of the Taínos, the original natives of the island. Pigeons stood guard all around the edges of the house's roof. Dogs ran to their car as they arrived, barking, growling or just grinning with tongues hanging out. One of the dogs had a crushed rear end with limp back legs dragging on the ground. Another had empty sockets where eyes had been. Another, pink scalded-looking skin. A tiny dog at the back of the pack kept opening his mouth as if to bark but no sound came out at all.

The priestess, the Behique, came tripping down the stone steps of the house to the yard below where Eliseo, Joanna and all the other guests were gathered waiting for her and for the bride and groom. The Behique wore a long white translucent gown revealing a golden brown curvaceous body underneath. Her thick white hair was in one long braid down her back, a silver bird's claw clinging to her chest, mother-of-pearl earrings radiating a silvery light. Right behind her came the bride and groom dressed in white tunics, chains of conch shells and crowned by feathered, beaded headbands. Everyone formed a circle around the three of them.

The Behique chanted, "We must always look for all the eyes, the infant eyes, vibrant ones, dying and dead eyes, even the eyes of our enemies. We must use them to see better, to see more and more. We must gather wisdom at every step. What is wisdom? It is to see with our inner eyes, to accept what we see and to heal where healing is needed." The pigeons began to coo even louder. The dogs howled like wolves except for the mute one. The priestess continued chanting, "Here we see two disparate souls, two disparate bodies coming together in a union of opposites that are but one." She sang of the merging, the blending, the balancing of all diverse energies, of earth and sky, life and death, the inner and outer world of all humans, of imagination and reality.

"The blending of imagination and reality," Joanna murmured to herself. Finally the couple was pronounced husband and wife and before long, after embracing everyone in the circle, they said goodbye and started their long walk up the mountain to a shack they had built together in the few days before the ceremony. Everyone then proceeded to the arbor where the Behique's helper from the nearby village had laid out a banquet of meats, beans, fruits, vegetables and a non-alcoholic cider.

Eliseo and Joanna sat quietly, hardly eating at all, their thighs, hips and upper arms touching. They no longer wondered why they were together. They knew at last. The Behique had seen it all; she had said it all.

After dinner their bountiful hostess gave each of them a small wooden pipe filled with what she called a magical powder. She then lit the pipes one by one with reverence as if bestowing a blessing. She said that all of them were of an age where they must try to resolve what up to now had been unresolved.

As Joanna huffed and puffed everyone laughed because she wasn't inhaling. It was something she had never learned to do. It felt good to have everyone smile at her allowing her to feel like a child, though she also wondered if perhaps in some way she had never quite grown up.

As Joanna created a shroud of mist around herself, no longer feeling her usual aches and pains and stiffness, she glided up a long staircase toward a blinding light. Was it similar to the one appearing right before death? Was she going to receive the revelation of her lifetime?

At the end of the luminosity she saw a brown skinned woman with thick long black hair. She was naked with opulent breasts, round belly, no hair on her pubis with her indentation wide open.

She was a priestess, a goddess.

"Tell me what you see," she said in Spanish. "*¿Qué es lo que ves?*"

"*Nada*," she answered. "I only see you."

"What do you hear?"

"I hear a song coming from far away. I hear the words of the jaguar from my mother's homeland. 'I am who I was always meant to be. No one can change the circular swirls of my body, the greenish moons of my eyes, the globules of silvery saliva that stream from my jowls.'"

"What does this mean to you?" The goddess queried.

"That the jaguar can never experience what it is like to be a plumed serpent, a kaleidoscopic quetzal bird, a multi-colored or an androgynous human being. She is simple, limited, curtailed, cheated by fate. It makes me sad."

"Do you see yet another scene, hear another song?"

"Yes," Joanna answered, "A woman is humming as she walks softly into a garden, not wanting to disturb all the crawling, creeping, flying things in the grass, in the bushes and in the trees. She goes straight to a pond, crouches down on her heels and begins to sing in a low hoarse voice in the same tone, in the same tempo as the frogs, only she is singing words."

"Does she make you feel sad also, like the jaguar did?" The deity asked.

"Yes, the woman is not adding to life or taking from it. She's just going with the flow, not transforming anything or being transformed."

"But didn't she add a little melody of her own to the scene?"

"Perhaps," Joanna said hesitantly.

"Do you think it is better to be more malleable like yourself with a gift for assuming many diverse roles?"

"I don't know," Joanna murmured suddenly feeling criticized, alone, belonging nowhere and to nobody, absolutely bereft. She looked directly at the splendid woman as she squatted back on her heels, knees and thighs far apart. She looked so receptive. Joanna didn't want any more songs; they were tiring her out with their certitude, their self-assuredness. She just wanted to waft up to the goddess, to enter her with her whole being, her whole nebulous being. She wanted to disappear within her, never to gain a form, never to be born.

As if she knew what Joanna had been thinking she said, "No, *mi querida hija*, my dear daughter, you cannot come back to me. You cannot hide anymore in closets, caves, costumes, in the veils you create, in the disease that—and this will shock you for you've spent your whole long life running away from me—you can't hide in the disease that keeps you within my arm's length with its' restrictions, its' constrictions on your movements."

As the golden light was extinguished, as the deity faded away and Joanna returned to the room full of food, drink and friends, she could only envy the proud jaguar and yearn for the humility of the woman singing with the frogs.

The Return of the Claw

Joanna's date had had to leave the bar suddenly, saying he needed to get home. That was fine with her really, although she was surprised, a bit crestfallen since they'd been getting on so well. "I'll walk you to the next corner," he said as if trying to be a little gallant.

"Fine," she answered thinking that at least she hadn't totally turned him off. They started out walking side by side, he, taller, stronger, trimmer. She was lame, one of her ankles and a foot refusing to limber up. Little by little they were out of sync as inch by inch he moved ahead of her leaving her lagging behind. It was difficult to talk to him. She was getting more and more breathless. She had wanted to ask him many things, especially what he'd thought of her years ago when they had known each other peripherally from workshops on psychology. She hadn't had the nerve to ask him in the bar; he was the kind of intellectual with a precise incisive mind that had always intimidated her, making her feel inferior. She had thought that when she learned more, got older, certainly when she was old that she'd get over feeling like this. "Please, Edwin, slow down. I can't walk as fast as you!"

"I'm sorry," he mumbled, slowing up momentarily only to speed up again almost immediately, his sense of purpose propelling him onwards, blinding him to her plight. Finally arriving at their destination as he turned to embrace her goodbye as if they'd had a nice stroll together, she had blurted out with a laugh, "You're the kind of man who needs the woman to walk behind him!" As if hearing something witty, he'd chuckled genially as he speeded off waving at her with his bad hand, his deformed hand wherein his five fingers had been reconstructed into two prongs, one longer than the other, a form of a talon. She hadn't had the chance to ask him how it happened—she assumed in some war long ago. "Funny," she thought, "his hand, my foot, two deformities that bound us together, 'birds of a feather' as they say." But though she tried to regain her equilibrium of spirit, she couldn't. She had to finally admit to herself that she felt belittled, humiliated, crushed.

As she slowly limped home, her mind began to go off on its own, not disciplined in the way of the intellectual, but needing to free itself of the confines of rationality, even of reality. Perhaps it merely needed to escape. She began to remember a television movie she'd seen ages ago. She didn't remember the story exactly, but it was part of a science fiction series dealing with the supernatural, the uncanny and paranormal. The setting was South America, possibly Argentina. A handsome older man, tall, elegant though wearing a somewhat threadbare suit, walked along the narrow alleyways of a large town followed by a skinny man with bleak eyes and a pointed beard—biblical-looking, some kind of a Job. The tall man suddenly stopped, confronting the little one, "Why are you following me, who are you?"

"I follow because I think I know you. You walk the way he did, you turn around in one swift movement, you almost seem to click your heels."

"You're crazy. I'm not whom you think I am. I would never have known the likes of you. Get away from me!"

"Yes, yes, the same cold rage, the arrogant irritation, the disdainful dismissive wave of the arm—you are he."

"Who are you talking about, you imbecile?"

"You are a cruel tormenter, a menace to the world, but you think yourself superior."

"Oh, get away, get away!" And the tall man began to run as fast as he could. The small man quickened his pace as if to follow but then stopped, smiling sadly to himself. There was no way he could catch up with the other.

In the next scene the tall man was seen seated on a bench in a museum staring at a painting of someone in a rowboat on a peaceful still river. The man in the picture, a blissful expression on his face, seemed to be surveying the tranquility, the beauty of the greenness of the water, of the surrounding trees. Day after day the tall man went to the museum, where he would sit for hours looking at the man in the rowboat. The shadow of the little man lurked in a corner observing him, absorbed in an inferno of his own that he couldn't shake but wished he could.

One day in a dream the tall man was told that if he wished hard enough with a pure heart while looking at his favorite painting he could be transported into the scene and thus be able to acquire a new life of absolute peace. He woke up in the middle of the night and impatient to start all over again, he hurried to the museum, broke in and in total darkness found his bench, taking for granted his painting was on the wall in front of him.

In the last scene, once again in the museum, there were two paintings spotlighted. One was of the rowboat on the glimmering river, the little man now sitting in it, his face aglow. The other painting, the one in front of the bench, was a rendition of *Dante's Inferno* by William Blake with a man forever burning to death, a man with the horrified tormented face of the tall man. Of course the paintings had been switched.

As Joanna had continued stumbling home on the uneven pavement with all its eruptions, upheavals of stone, feeling more and more dizzy, sick at heart, she had felt as if she were in a giant painting whose images within were rendered in a circular fashion. She stood in the center with Edwin pulling her along by the hair with his pincer-like hand, her foot looking like a cloven hoof. In the next circle around them swirled the tall man and the little man from the television movie, both reaching for the elusive river waters with its reflections of peace and beauty while pursued by hellish devouring flames. The last circle, the outer circle had been

190

dim at first, not well lit, very still, unmoving. Big and little objects. Dark and light objects. Big things on top of little ones. Then they had begun to move as the objects took on a human form, human faces. There she was, young, long-legged, light-skinned, leaping ahead of the others, ahead of her short-legged, tiny footed Indian mother and her two swarthy younger sisters. "I must run, run ahead, I don't belong with you, it's all a mistake; let me not be seen with you lest I have to be like you; I'm different, of another clan, another world, a better place!"

"Espéranos por favor, wait for us!" they pleaded with dismay, but to no avail.

By the time Joanna got home that evening practically dragging her feet behind her, prodded onwards by an invisible claw, a reconstructed hand, she knew the true meaning of expressions like "what goes around, comes around." Yes, the winged demons had come full circle.

The Domain of the Sycamore

The old tree was just over the fence in the neighbor's backyard, but its towering height made it omnipresent. Of course it'd been there during all of Joanna's previous visits to her sister's house in the outskirts of London, England but for some reason it had never called to her the way it was calling to her now. Its restless voice sang to her outside the window of the guestroom, and as soon as she went out into the garden its branches slowly swayed in her direction. Perhaps it called to her because she was now an old woman.

One evening she went outside to the patio at seven o'clock because she knew the homing pigeons from down the lane would be out for their nightly exercises. As she stretched her body down on the chair, resting her head on its back, she watched the fifteen or twenty pigeons beginning their circles up high and slowly flying lower and lower. She liked to think that they were paying homage to the old Sycamore, the tallest tree in the neighborhood. A few moments later Ana joined her bringing two gin and tonics which she placed on the table before sitting down. Straightening herself up and taking a long sip as if consumed by thirst, Joanna gestured toward the Sycamore, "Aren't you worried that when your neighbor leaves or dies the new owners will cut down that beautiful tree?"

"Are you joking? I hope they do! That tree is a horror—its roots guzzle up tons of water from the ground!"

"So? What's wrong with that? It's been around long enough to deserve it."

Ana put down her glass as she fixed her enormous dark eyes

on Joanna, the corners of her lips turned downwards, her grayish-black hair seeming to stand on end, "For your information its monstrous roots are undermining the foundation of my house, my home!"

"Can it really do that? It's not even that close!"

"I know, I know, but those damn roots are reaching for my cottage!"

After taking another long sip of her drink trying to suppress her laughter, knowing that Ana hated any semblance of mockery, Joanna cautiously murmured, "Oh really? I'm sorry but I only see an old tall tree full of dry leaves and knots and cracks."

"No, it's a nasty tree—its branches have horrible green worms that keep falling onto my side of the fence, killing off anything they fall on!"

"That's funny; I've gone up real close and I've never seen any worms, only a yellow-green vine encircling its trunk."

"Of course! If vipers were dangling from every branch you wouldn't see a thing!"

Sinking back down on her seat Joanna thought she'd not respond. With her eyes closed she wrapped her ample caftan tightly around her arms, wondering if she should at least make some kind of diverting remark. Perhaps she could point out that the ginger-colored cat sitting on the gray roof at the foot of the garden had been staring at them all evening. Perhaps she could ask Ana if she'd ever eaten any of the apples growing in her very own tree.

Then after a few moments Joanna couldn't help but break the silence, "Are you trying to tell me something? Ever since I arrived you've seemed far off, moody."

"What do you mean?" Ana's eyes looked aggrieved as if Joanna were criticizing her.

Joanna sighed, feeling once again pushed into the role of the older sister, "You seem resentful as if you're biting your tongue, as if there's something you want to say that you've never been able to say before."

"Like what?" Ana asked.

"How would I know! You're the one always holding on to old grievances!" Joanna answered impatiently, unwrapping herself and drinking from her glass as she looked up at the Sycamore, listening to the rustling of its leaves.

"See, that's what I hate; you're always trying to tell me what I'm thinking or feeling! Why should I still be upset about the past? Then squashing her spiky hair down at the top of her head Ana added, "Anyway, dinner's almost ready; let's just finish our drink and talk about something else!"

For a few minutes nothing further was said. Yellow butterflies flitted nervously around them, going from plant to plant as if looking for something. As Joanna looked at them she remembered Ana telling her long ago that the bushes had all been planted to commemorate something, the death of the family dog, her divorce, her grown-up children moving away, the end of an affair. Had some of the other palms, aromatic herbs and ferns with red berries been given life in memory of other losses, other disillusionments? Losing Joanna to an early marriage in New York, further losing her to the family's move to another continent, still further losing her to her subsequent refusals to rejoin the family in England? Perhaps the last straw had been Joanna enticing their youngest sister long, long ago to move back to New York, thus forever dividing the family into two camps, into what Ana called the cocky Americans and the stick-in-the-mud English.

Finally Joanna said, "I can almost see a little quail nestling at the foot of the Sycamore, a puffy lovely thing painted like a tabby cat with orange eye shadow. No, I see two of them, two quails sitting close to each other."

Ana laughed and then smiling she murmured, "Make it two partridges instead of two quails because the partridge is not a migrant like the quail."

"Okay, two partridges who stay put! I like that image," Joanna said reaching for Ana's hand which rested nearby on the table.

Allowing her sister to stroke her hand Ana continued, "Now, don't jump down my throat but I can't help but see you as a pheasant up on top of the tree, your long elegant tail hanging down, your head plumes blowing in the breeze. You flutter your wings as you call out to the puffy partridges down below."

Joanna squeezed Ana's hand really hard and held onto it as she tried to stop tears from welling up in her eyes. Then laughing she said, "Well, all these birds have something in common; can you guess what?"

Wincing, trying gently to disengage her hand from Joanna's, Ana asked, "No, what?"

"They're all game, wild or tame, migrant or not, lofty or not, they're still just game birds!"

As Joanna released her hand Ana chuckled, "And on that happy note let's go and eat our dinner!"

"Yes!" Joanna exclaimed looking up at the old tree one more time, "I'm famished!" She saw that the homing pigeons were doing their last circle, flying just over the top of the Sycamore as they headed back to their master and their cages. "Nothing ever changes, does it?" Joanna asked to no one in particular.

FERRETING IN THE BURROWS

He was some sort of terrier, bushy eyebrows, long lashes, generally whiskered like a gentleman of long ago. But he was old, his hips frozen, his hearing just about gone. His name doesn't matter, only that he and Joanna were left together in a lodge in Estes Park, Colorado as the others, their family, went hiking in the Rocky Mountains. As for Joanna it was her anklebones that were frozen in place. She lay down on the bed on her side looking at the icy branches of the Ponderosa trees hoping a family of deer would walk past the wide window as they already had many times in the past few days of their holiday visit, their alert tails held high exposing immaculate tan-colored behinds. She knew that if she stood up she might see an elk or two across the frozen stream. But she didn't want to move, for, in addition to her ankles, everything hurt, bent bones, sagging muscles, twisted tendons and ligaments. As she chucked to herself she wondered if it mattered to her that she was no longer beautiful. Did it bother her that she had had rheumatoid arthritis for over forty years? Did she feel sorry for herself, no, not in a weepy whiny way but in an empathetic realistic way? With a shock she realized that she truly didn't know. Why didn't she know? How had she reached old age having studied psychology and been a practicing psychotherapist and not know?

The gray beast on the rug by the bed raised his head picking up his grisly pointed ears as if, despite his deafness, he heard something far off in the distance. She heard nothing. He struggled up, heading for the window dragging his hind legs, his tail wagging with agitation. Did he hear the murmuring of the wind or the distant voices of the wild? After a few moments, he returned to her side, snuffling a little as he curled up into a tight circle, his glistening black nose coming to rest on his long crooked toes, one ear up and one folded down as if not sure he wanted to sense anything at all.

What was it one of the nurses had said to Joanna twenty years ago as she had bathed her in bed following the surgical fusion of her neck vertebrae? "I don't know how you can just keep going!" Joanna had been astounded. She hadn't been aware that her life, that is, the medical records of her life, even with the many joint replacements and reconstructions, looked so bad. It didn't feel that bad to her.

The terrier's head popped up once again, his nose up in the air, the black band down the middle of his back quivering as the surrounding gray hairs fluffed up just a bit. Slowly he rose once again and headed for the window, this time beginning to whimper as he trembled more violently. Perturbed by his agitation a shiver ran through Joanna. Maybe he was in pain; maybe he was dying. "Shhh…!" she tried to calm him, "Shhh…be quiet! There's nothing out there. They won't be back for hours!"

To no avail—he began to wail, a long lingering lamentation. Was he bemoaning having been left behind, left and perhaps abandoned? Is that how she had felt sometimes? Soon after an image began to form, an image of being thrown aside, thrown off her ornamental chair, dethroned. More images followed—father embracing her fervently while at the same time pulling away, leaving to go overseas—then much later father crying while at the same time telling her by telephone that he and the whole family were moving away from her to live in Europe. No, enough! She was tired of all that! It happened so long ago.

By now the terrier was in a frenzy, his head raised, howling up into the glass window, through it and beyond, up the mountain, shaking the snow off the tree branches, frightening the magpies with their black and white simplicity, causing the ptarmigans to turn their feathers brown, then white again, not knowing whether it was the summer or the winter, piercing the ears of the mountain cats stopping them in their tracks right before they pounced on their prey.

Beginning to shiver Joanna got under the blankets. Still shaking, she fell asleep, lullabyed by the dog's sing-song wail. When she awoke, she was no longer cold and the terrier was asleep.

Their family would be back soon. That night they were to celebrate the New Year. She knew that besides warmly toasting each other in front of a roaring fire, she would make a secret toast to her disease, rheumatoid arthritis, for, though hopefully, she didn't need it any more, she *had* needed it. She had perhaps even loved it as a friend. It had been her protest, her howl of anguish, her voice.

Joanna was in a cottage at Gleesk Pier in southwest Ireland high up in what felt like a tree-house. She overlooked a desolate scene, craggy boulders and an icy expanse of water. Green shrubs sprout wherever they can, competing with the cracked jagged rocks, their prickly nature covered by pretty little lavender and yellow flowers. The clouds cast dark shadows upon the South Channel inlet waters which lie quietly, not making waves, preferring to be a mirror, a glistening recorder of its environs.

In her reverie she may not even be human. Perhaps she's still within an egg. Perhaps she's soon to be realized as a gull, a black-headed gull with an orange beak. In her reverie she hears voices coming from far, far away. She sees distant images of another land.

"Don't touch the eggs in the nest!" It is the voice of their grandmother talking to their mother when she was a little girl in Mexico.

"Porque no?"

"Because you'll contaminate them!" continues *abuela* in a severe tone.

"What does that mean?" their mother asks in a subdued voice.

"You'll put a scent on them that might render them an easy prey."

Joanna's mother still didn't understand but as usual she was too afraid to ask any further questions. In any case how could her little hands do anything as dire as what she sensed in her mother's voice? So one day after thoroughly washing her hands with a pumice stone she rushed to the tallest tree in the countryside, far away from her little house in her small town. It was an ancient multi-trunked cypress. She climbed from one forked ledge to another, higher and higher. Looking down she saw all the puffy marigolds looking up at her. At the top she found the nest she was looking for, a large round woven basket made of thick twigs. Inside were four polka-dotted brown eggs, having the same color and markings as the bark of the cypress. She knew that within each egg was the beginning of a large bird who would need the height of the old tree in order to first try out its wide wings. Her fingers ached to hold the eggs but she couldn't just yet, her hands having gotten dirty climbing the tree. She licked each segment of each finger slowly, thoroughly. Then feeling pure, pristine, certain her mother would approve, she picked up first one egg and then the other, rolling them gently around in the palms of her hands. Then she put each one right up to her mouth, kissing them lightly with pursed-up shiny lips, before she skidded more than climbed down from her heights singing to herself, *"Los pajaritos son mios; son mis hijos!"* (The little birds are mine; they are my children.) Little did she know she was to have four children with Joanna's father, three daughters and a son who died as an infant.

She didn't tell *abuela* of her excursion. She believed with all her being that she would prove her mother wrong; she would prove that there was nothing wrong with her, with her hands, that they couldn't possibly do anything bad to the spotted eggs. A few days later she climbed back up the tree, eager to see the newly hatched eggs. Up, up she went almost floating upwards, so familiar was she with the old cypress. She even closed her eyes so she'd get a stronger visual impact upon opening them. Resting on a ledge she pressed her fists tightly against her eyeballs creating a picture of sparkling stars and black moons.

Opening her eyes she couldn't believe what she saw—a spiraling rounded pyramid sitting upon the bird nest, its peak quickly rearing up to face her, hissing a possessive warning. It was a coiled up snake. A terrible shriek broke out above her head. Looking up she saw a large black-headed bird standing on a branch, fiercely flapping its white-fringed wings, its orange-yellow eyes flashing wildly, its dagger-like beak preparing to descend upon the serpent. In Joanna's reverie she could feel the rage of the bird, the fright, the agony over the plight of the poor fledglings, herself and her two younger sisters, no longer young but forever with the mark of the snake upon them.

But now as Joanna the bird-woman of two worlds, the Mexican and the Irish, looked around at the terrain that belonged to their father and his clan long, long ago, she saw that the sun was shining upon each and every boulder, each thistle with its lavender flower, each buckhorn with its star-like yellow blossom, each lumbering sheep with its black booties, each with its face masked as if on the way to a grand ball. The waters are now a rippling gold and silver, the white clouds lounging deities. Where are the contaminating hands, the prey with their predators? They're gone. Forever do you think?